TARAS BULBA

Nikolai Gogol

Taras Bulba

A new translation by Peter Constantine

Introduction by Robert D. Kaplan

THE MODERN LIBRARY

NEW YORK

2003 Modern Library Edition

Biographical note copyright © 1997 by Random House, Inc.
Translation copyright © 2003 by Random House, Inc.
Introduction copyright © 2003 by Robert D. Kaplan

LIBRARY OF CONGRESS CATALOGING-IN-PUBLICATION DATA
Gogol, Nikolai Vasil'evich, 1809–1852.
[Taras Bul'ba. English]
Taras Bulba / Nikolai Gogol; translated by Peter Constantine,
with an introduction by Robert D. Kaplan.
p.   cm.
ISBN 0-679-64255-2
I. Constantine, Peter, 1963–   II. Kaplan, Robert D., 1952–   III. Title.
PG3333 .T3 2003
891.73'3—dc21   2002032595

Modern Library website address: www.modernlibrary.com

Printed in the United States of America on acid-free paper

2 4 6 8 9 7 5 3 1

Nikolai V. Gogol

Nikolai Gogol, whose imaginative, satiric work ushered in the naturalist movement in Russian literature, was born in the Ukrainian town of Sorochintsy on April 1, 1809 (March 19 by the Russian calendar), into a family of ancient and noble Cossack lineage. His father was a minor official, amateur playwright, and gentleman farmer who presided over Vassilyevka, an estate of some three thousand acres where Gogol grew up in an atmosphere of relative affluence and parental indulgence. In 1821, at the age of twelve, Gogol left Vassilyevka and entered the School of Higher Studies at Nezhin; there he developed an unbridled passion for theater and poetry. After he graduated in 1828, he attempted to find work as an actor but also published *Hans Kuechelgärten* (1829), an epic poem that received only negative reviews. He secured a post with a government ministry in St. Petersburg and began writing a series of folktales set in his native Ukraine.

The appearance of *Evenings on a Farm Near Dikanka* in 1831 brought Gogol immediate acclaim. "I have finished reading *Evenings,*" wrote

Alexander Pushkin to a friend. "An astounding book! Here is fun for you, authentic fun of the frankest kind without anything maudlin or prim about it. And moreover—what poetry, what delicacy of sentiment in certain passages! All this is so unusual in our literature that I am still unable to get over it."

Gogol's association with Pushkin soon inspired two of his greatest works: the play *The Inspector General* and *Dead Souls*. A comedy of mistaken identity that is a satiric indictment of Russian bureaucracy, *The Inspector General* set all of Russia laughing when it was staged in 1836. "Everyone has got his due, and I most of all," Tsar Nicholas I reportedly remarked. "*The Inspector General* happened to be the greatest play ever written in Russian (and never surpassed since)," judged Vladimir Nabokov. "The play begins with a blinding flash of lightning and ends in thunderclap. In fact it is wholly placed in the tense gap between the flash and the crash. . . . Gogol's play is poetry in action."

Stung by criticism of *The Inspector General*, Gogol moved to Italy in 1836, and except for two brief visits home he remained abroad for twelve years. Much of this time was devoted to writing *Dead Souls*. Published in 1842, the novel revolves around Pavel Ivanovich Chichikov, a mystifying swindler who travels through provincial Russia trafficking in "souls"—serfs who, despite being dead, could still be bought and sold.

The same year marked the appearance of Gogol's famous short story "The Overcoat," in which a buffoonish clerk is robbed of a symbolic garment that represents all his hopes and dreams. "We all came from Gogol's 'Overcoat,' " said Dostoevsky in acknowledgment of Russian literature's vast debt to Gogol. And Vladimir Nabokov noted: "When, as in his immortal 'The Overcoat,' Gogol really let himself go and pottered happily on the brink of his private abyss, he became the greatest artist that Russia has yet produced." But *Selected Passages from Correspondence with My Friends* (1847), a reactionary work reflecting the writer's growing religious and moral fanaticism, virtually ended his career.

Nikolai Gogol · vii

Gogol spent his final years struggling in vain to finish the second part of *Dead Souls:* a sequel in which he intended to depict Chichikov's moral conversion. The effort helped propel him into insanity, and he burned the final version of the manuscript shortly before his death in Moscow, following weeks of fasting, on the morning of March 4, 1852 (February 21 by the Russian calendar). Commenting on the crowd at Gogol's funeral, a passerby asked: "Who is this man who has so many relatives at his funeral?" A mourner replied: "This is Nikolai Gogol, and all of Russia is his relative."

CONTENTS

Introduction

Euphorias of Hatred:
The Grim Lessons of a Novel by Gogol

Robert D. Kaplan

The ancient Greeks, it has been said, were too reasonable to ignore the intoxicating power of the unreasonable. They worshiped Dionysus, the god of excess and ecstasy, and they admired tragedy—an art form that shows how human feelings are far too intense and varied to fit into the gray, narrow strictures of rational self-interest. Explosions of passion—romantic and destructive, cruel and self-sacrificing, among nations as among individuals—not only are to be expected but are central to the human spirit. Tragedy, as the classicist Edith Hamilton once observed, is the beauty of intolerable truths.

The signal error of the American elite after the end of the Cold War was its trust in rationalism, which, it was assumed, would eventually propel the world's peoples toward societies based on individual rights, united by American-style capitalism and technology. Recent explanations for terrorism have likewise been excessively rational. In the immediate aftermath of the attacks on the United States, many commentators and academics asserted that terrorism stemmed from poverty. Then, looking more closely, they said it stemmed from rising expectations and perceived inequalities. True enough: economic development often leads to upheaval and insurrection, as urban migration and the rise of the middle class unleash all manner of ambitions and yearnings. But even if poverty and perceived inequality were to vanish, and the rough places in the road of development were made plain, depraved outrages would continue. The more advanced a civilization, the more cerebral and subtly conformist it is likely to be—and, consequently, the more extreme the pent-up frustration that becomes the source of spectacular violence.

———

If realism is to be truly realistic, it must acknowledge the romantic and heroic impulses in human beings, in all their healthy and perverse forms. Few writers do this as economically as Nikolai Vasilievich Gogol did in *Taras Bulba*. This short novel is a story of the Dnieper Cossacks. It takes place in a hazy past, sometime between the mid-sixteenth and early seventeenth century, when the Ukrainians are struggling for independence from Poland even as a threat persists from the Turks. It is a work that the critic John Cournos likens to a Homeric epic, "filled with as much Dionysian hate and heroism as the *Iliad*." The work has a Kiplingesque gusto, too, that makes it a pleasure to read, but central to its theme is an unredemptive, darkly evil violence that is far beyond anything Kipling ever touched on. We need more works like *Taras Bulba*, to better understand the emotional wellsprings of the threat we face today in places like the Middle East and Central Asia.

Gogol gave his best years to the story—he finished the initial version in 1835 and the final version a decade later. According to David Magarshack, one of Gogol's translators, *Taras Bulba* is the work that, with its romantic evocation of galloping Cossacks, created the myth of the "Russian soul." But Gogol was no dreamy idealist: in *Taras Bulba* he writes of a "grim era in which man, living a blood-drenched life of military campaigns, tempered his soul by stifling his humanity."

Gogol was a Russian nationalist but he saw the real, primordial

Russia in the Ukraine (a word meaning "Borderland"), whose un-remitting and unimpeded steppes—lacking natural boundaries and drained by few navigable rivers—had made its colliding peoples war-like. Although Gogol used the words "Russian," "Ukrainian," and "Cossack" to denote specific identities, he also recognized that these identities greatly overlapped (as local identities still do). His account mirrors the conflicts, the confusions, and the nuances of our own era. It remains unclear, for instance, whether Ukraine will survive as an in-dependent country or at some point will dissipate within the pressure cooker of a resurgent Russian Empire.

In Gogol's account, the absence of natural boundaries leaves the Ukrainian steppes open to invaders from all sides. It also makes politi-cal frontiers artificial. Compare Central Asia today: a seething table-land of calcified regimes and nationalities inside false borders. Ethnic Tajiks dominate the great cities of Uzbekistan. Ethnic Uzbeks com-prise a quarter of the population of Tajikistan. The great divisions in Gogol's *Taras Bulba* are those of civilizations: the Eastern Orthodox Dnieper Cossacks are pitted against the Catholic Poles and the Mus-lim Turks and Tatars. This is a world so coarse, and so unreceptive to enlightenment, that freedom means only the freedom to express one-self through a stultifying yet energizing group identity—a sad com-monplace in many parts of the world today, where dictatorships are crumbling and real democracy is weak or nonexistent. In such places, a fury burns that is beyond the cultivated bourgeois imagination. Gogol communicates this fury brilliantly.

Taras Bulba, a Dnieper Cossack, is an old regular army colonel. He is a man, in Gogol's words, "made for the alarms of war [who] stood out for the rough straightforwardness of his temper." Taras abuses his wife, who he fears will soften the character of his two sons. His worst nightmare is that his sons will never experience violence: he doesn't care if they die young and horribly, so long as they prove themselves capable of cruelty against an enemy.

Gogol explains that a fearsome character like Taras could only be forged out of the chaos that had engulfed southern Russia, "abandoned by its princes [and] laid waste and left in ruins by the relentless . . . Mongol marauders." A treeless landscape of charred villages stretched for hundreds of miles. Deprived of security—indeed, of any real government—and surrounded by predatory neighbors, men became cruel and fearless. In response the Cossack brotherhoods emerged, with their apotheosis of "comradeship." Private, material life came to be considered shameful. Russian communism may be better understood less as an import from Central European intellectuals than as a reflection of Russia's own inherent psychologial tendencies. (According to the Russian intellectual Nicolas Berdyaev, Bolshevism was the Eastern Orthodox form of Marxism, in that it was a faith imbued with the idea of "totality.")

For the Dnieper Cossacks in *Taras Bulba,* violence is a way of life, an expression of joy and belief, unlinked to any strategic or tactical necessity. Warfare in the novel is nearly continuous. As one Cossack declares, "as we all know, a young man cannot make do without war." In such a world any notion of a rational "balance of power" with the Catholic Poles or the Islamic Tatars is not a pragmatic goal but a corrupting and effeminate conceit. Those outside the marrow of Orthodoxy exist only to be annihilated, or to be converted en masse to the faith.

Because the intervals between fighting are rare, they are also precious, and are given over to "spellbinding"—that is, to prolonged drunken orgies. "Stores were ransacked," Gogol writes, "of mead, vodka, and beer, and the storekeepers were glad to escape with their lives." Hearing stories of Catholic victories to the west, and of Jewish collusion in those victories, the Cossacks take murderous revenge on local Jews, whom they toss into the river.

Gogol's Cossacks represent the ultimate crowd-pack, fueled by the crude belief systems and symbolism that sustain what the national security analyst Ralph Peters has called "euphorias of hatred." Peters notes that although individual people are equally capable of love and hate, crowds are incomparably better at hatred. Individuals within a crowd are able to take part in cathartic violence without having to accept responsibility for it. The crowd that cheered in Ramallah in October 2000 as two Israeli soldiers were tortured and defenestrated is a classic example of this.

Elias Canetti, the Bulgarian-born Nobel laureate who devoted a career to the study of crowds, has written, "The crowd needs a direction.... Its constant fear of disintegration means that it will accept any goal." There's no reasoning with a crowd, in other words: against the absolute faith of a Cossack horde, for example, the urban civilization of the Poles is nothing. This kind of faith, Gogol writes, is "insurmountable and ferocious, like a rock rising from the depths of a stormy ocean, fashioned from a single unshatterable mass of stone."

———

The raw, even delusional, passion at the heart of such faith has played a frightful role in human affairs. One need look no further than the devastation brought about in twentieth-century Europe by the crowd-pack to understand the destructive power that this passion can unleash. And yet, ironically, meeting the challenge of the crowd-pack—indeed, even surviving as a society—requires a willingness to tap into the same dangerously elemental energies of raw passion. Channeled effectively, these energies can also become the wellspring of liberal patriotism, heroism, and romance.

This kind of passion remains robust in the United States—a firm conclusion one can draw from our post–9/11 stocktaking. Foreigners often find Americans as a group more than a little hard to take, put off by the overt nationalism, the deep religiosity, the proud vulgarity, the searing public debate, the unashamed sentimentality, the battered but defiant idealism. These are precisely the qualities that are disappearing in Europe. Traumatized by world war and absolutist political ideology, Western Europe's political elites have been working for decades to neutralize passion altogether. Europe's intellectuals and politicians have become increasingly effete, bureaucratic, and defeatist; their foreign policies, to the extent that they even exist, amount to a form of regulatory compromise, guaranteed to pursue the path of least resistance. Europe, if it seeks to avoid decline, will have to relearn the lesson of Gogol and the ancient Greeks: that rational argument alone will never fully overcome those who simply and passionately believe.

———

ROBERT D. KAPLAN is a correspondent for *The Atlantic Monthly* and the author of nine books on travel and foreign affairs, including *Balkan Ghosts, Eastward to Tartary, The Ends of the Earth,* and *The Coming Anarchy.* His tenth book, *Mediterranean Winter,* will be published by Random House next year. He lives with his wife and son in western Massachusetts.

Translator's Preface

Peter Constantine

"That splendid epic worthy of Homer . . . that colossal portrait in a small frame," wrote the Russian critic Belinsky about *Taras Bulba* when it first appeared in 1835. Published initially in the form of a long story when Gogol was twenty-six, it was one of his most successful early works. He then went on to develop it over the next six years into the more mature and complex novel published in 1842, the version used for this translation.

Gogol had burst onto the Russian literary scene in 1831 with a volume of stories, *Evenings on a Farm Near the Dikanka River,* a second volume of which appeared a year later. In January 1835, he published a two-volume collection of stories, *Arabeski,* followed in March of the same year by another two-volume story collection, *Mirgorod,* in which the first version of *Taras Bulba* appeared.

These early works reflect Gogol's deep interest in his native Ukraine, with its rich folklore and Cossack traditions. The stories, mainly folk-inspired tales mixing naturalism and fantasy, focus almost exclusively on Ukrainian themes, the natural beauty of the steppes, and the historic struggles of its people. Gogol's father, Vasily Afanasevich Gogol, had written plays in Ukrainian, which at the time was considered a substandard dialect of Russian, and Nikolai inherited his father's passion for the Ukrainian language and culture, and worked on a Ukrainian-Russian dictionary as well as gathering Ukrainian proverbs and sayings. Though his prose was affected by the Ukrainian language, particularly in the speech of his characters, Gogol always wrote in Russian.

Taras Bulba is Gogol's only completed historical work, an epic in prose that combines influences from Ukrainian ballads, Russian folk epics, the romances of Sir Walter Scott, and Homer's *Iliad*. Gogol took the Cossack way of life, with its traditions and warrior pride, and gave it an epic cast. Scott was a particularly important model, as Gogol could empathize with his quest to preserve Scotland's ballads and tales and to re-create its heroic sagas, and he found Scott's formula for historical fiction useful for re-creating the untamed Ukrainian past.

In the final version of *Taras Bulba*, Gogol emphasized Russian as opposed to Ukrainian patriotism, turning the wild Cossacks of the past into chivalric crusaders for the Russian Orthodox faith against the Polish Catholics who were striving to subjugate the Ukraine. The novel also presents a stark picture of the Cossacks' brutality toward the Jews. The later version of the novel also introduces specific Homeric devices that help elevate the novel's action, such as extended metaphors, the cataloging of the heroes' names, and similes that retard the action at crucial moments and heighten the tension. In one instance, Gogol describes Taras Bulba's heroic son Ostap at a critical moment on the battlefield to be "like a hawk flying wide circles high in the sky, its powerful wings spread wide, stopping suddenly before plummeting like an arrow at the quail squealing in terror." While in the *Iliad*, Homer describes Hector attacking Achilles "like a hawk which hovers awhile over some lofty cliff, then darts to earth after a bird."[1]

1. *The Iliad*, translated by W.H.D. Rouse (New York, 1960), p. 150.

Within the epic scope of *Taras Bulba,* Gogol presents a detailed picture of the structure and principles of the Sech (the fortified Cossack encampment) on an island in the river Dnieper. Gogol's description of the structure of the Sech is detailed and realistic, though historians have pointed out that he brought together historical elements from the sixteenth and seventeenth centuries for literary effect. This adds to the timeless quality of *Taras Bulba,* which is set, as Robert Kaplan points out in his Introduction, "sometime between the mid-sixteenth and seventeenth century."

The Cossacks were the descendants of disenfranchised Russians who, during the reign of Ivan the Great (1440–1505), migrated to the Ukraine in search of freedom during "the gathering of the lands"— Ivan's subjugation of the principalities surrounding Moscow to form a greater Muscovy. Over the next centuries, the Cossack communities fought for their continued independence, making their own laws and electing their own chiefs and commanders. By the mid-sixteenth century there were two large Cossack strongholds: one was on the river Don, the other was the Zaporozhian Sech on the Dnieper.

In the Zaporozhian Sech, unmarried Cossacks lived in fortified barracks from which women were excluded, while their married comrades—like Taras Bulba—lived in homesteads outside the Sech. The married Cossacks would regularly come to the Sech to join the Cossack army on campaigns and raids. Each year an assembly consisting of every adult Cossack elected a council of commanders to run the community's affairs and to choose a leader, the Ataman. As Gogol shows, the Ataman's powers were absolute during times of war, though the Ataman did convene assemblies to decide on important strategies. The assembly based its decisions on which Cossack faction shouted the loudest. Sometimes violence broke out during the voting.

The presence of the warring Cossacks on the western steppes of the Ukraine unsettled both the Polish and the Muscovite governments. Both tried to gain influence over the Cossacks by registering them, which made them subject to military duty. Taras Bulba "loved the simple life of the Cossack, and quarreled with comrades who were drawn to the Warsaw faction, accusing them of being lackeys of the Polish noblemen."

Gogol modeled Taras Bulba on Bogdan Khmelnitsky (1595–1657), who was Ataman of the Zaporozhian Cossacks from 1648 to 1657, and who organized a rebellion against Polish rule in the Ukraine that ultimately led to the transfer of the Ukrainian lands east of the Dnieper to Russian control.

In *Taras Bulba*, Gogol made the Cossacks the emblem of the Russian spirit:

> [T]he whole of primitive Russia's south, abandoned by its princes, was laid waste and left in ruins by the relentless onslaught of the Mongol marauders; it was a time when man, turned out of house and home, became dauntless, when he settled in charred ruins in the face of terrible neighbors and never-ending danger, learning to look them in the eye and unlearning that fear exists in the world; when the flames of war gripped the ancient peaceful Slavic spirit, and Cossackry—that wide, raging sweep of Russian character—was introduced. . . . It was truly an extraordinary phenomenon of Russian power, arising from the national heart of fiery poverty.

The style of *Taras Bulba* is unlike anything Gogol wrote before or after. The expansive epic tone is quite different from the sharp and witty social critique of his later works, such as *Dead Souls* or "The Overcoat." One of the major tasks facing this translator was to fathom and reflect Gogol's rendition of Cossack speech in its simplicity and directness, speech that nevertheless harbors a noble grandeur. Gogol's Cossacks are men of war who best express themselves in the violence of battle, and yet when they do speak, their words have an epic weight. I was fortunate to be able to rely on my Russian editor, Katya Ilina, who is of Cossack background and who was able to explain many details and nuances. I am thankful for the many hours she spent checking the text.

I would also like to express my thanks to MJ Devaney, my editor at Modern Library, and to my agent, Jessica Wainwright, whose interest in Russian literature has been a source of great encouragement over the years.

My very special thanks to Burton Pike, who introduced me to the pleasures of translation and who provided much advice and support throughout the project.

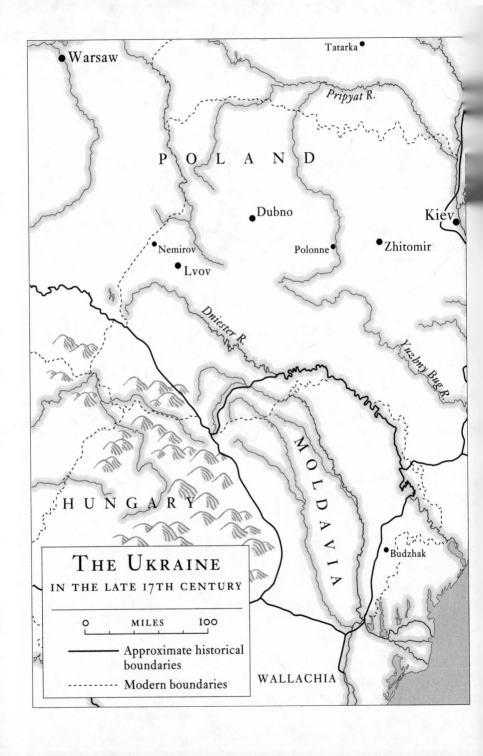

Warsaw

Tatarka

Pripyat R.

P O L A N D

Dubno

Kiev

Nemirov

Polonne

Zhitomir

Lvov

Dniester R.

Yuzhny Bug R.

H U N G A R Y

M O L D A V I A

Budzhak

THE UKRAINE
IN THE LATE 17TH CENTURY

0   MILES   100

——— Approximate historical
        boundaries
------- Modern boundaries

WALLACHIA

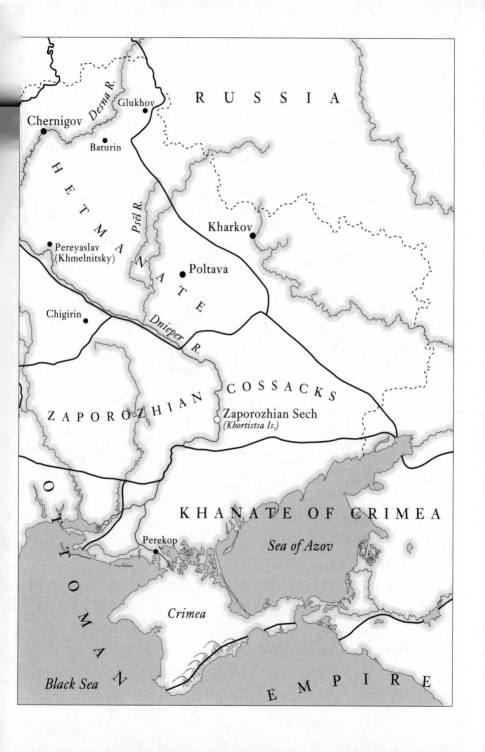

TARAS BULBA

1

"Turn around and let me look at you! What a sight! What are you wearing there, a priest's cassock or something? Is that how you run around at that academy of yours?"

These were the words with which old Bulba greeted his two sons, who, having completed their studies at the Seminary in Kiev, had come home to their father. The sons had just dismounted from their horses. They were robust young men, with the sullen look one sees in all Seminary students recently released. Their strong, healthy faces were covered with a first down that had not yet been touched by a razor. Embarrassed by the way their father welcomed them, they stared sullenly at the ground.

"Wait, wait! Let me get a good look at you!" Bulba continued, turning them around. "What are these long tunics you're wearing, if you can even call them that? I've never seen the like! Take a few steps—I swear they'll get caught between your legs, and you'll go flying!"

"Don't make fun of us, Papa!" the older of the boys finally said.

"Look how high and mighty he is! And why, pray, shouldn't I make fun of you?"

"Because, well ... even though you're my papa, if you make fun of me, then by God I'll thrash you!"

"Ha! You damn son of a you-know-what! Your own father?" Taras Bulba shouted, staggering back in surprise.

"Yes, even though you're my father. Insult me, and I don't care who you are!"

"So how do you want to fight, with your fists?"

"Any way you want!"

"Well then, show me your fists!" Taras Bulba said, pulling up his sleeves. "I'd like to see what kind of man you are with your fists!"

Father and son, instead of greeting one another after their long separation, began throwing punches at each other's stomach and chest, stepping back to glare at each other and then attacking again.

"Neighbors, villagers!" shouted the boys' pale, gaunt mother, who was standing on the threshold and had not had a chance to embrace her beloved children. "The old man's gone mad! His mind's unhinged! The boys come home, we haven't seen them for over a year, and what does he do? Fly at them with his fists!"

"He fights well, this one!" Bulba gasped, stopping for a moment. "By God, he fights well!" he continued, catching his breath. "So well that I'd have done better not to test him. He'll make a good Cossack, this one! I welcome you, my son! Let us kiss!"

And father and son kissed.

"Well done, my boy! You can get the better of any man if you go at him the way you went at me! Show mercy to no one. But I still think you're wearing the oddest clothes I've ever seen! What's this string hanging there? And you," he shouted, turning to his younger son. "You Grand Padishah, why are you standing there with your arms dangling?* You son of a dog, aren't you going to punch me too?"

* Padishah = "Great Emperor." The title of the sultan of Turkey.

"What will he think of next?" the mother gasped, throwing her arms around the boy. "He wants his own flesh and blood to raise a hand to him! That's all we need! The boy is young, has had a long journey, and must be exhausted!" (The boy was nearly twenty and well over six feet tall.) "He has to rest and eat a bite of food, and the old fool wants to fight him!"

"You're a milksop, I see!" Bulba said. "Don't listen to your mother, my boy! She's a woman, she knows nothing! What do you need sweetness for? An open field and a good horse, that's all the sweetness you need! You see this saber? This saber is your mother! They've been filling your heads with filth, that's what they've been doing! The Seminary, and all those little books and primers and philosophy and the devil knows what else—I spit on it all!" And Bulba slipped in a word that cannot appear in print. "What I ought to do is send you this very week to Zaporozhe.* That's where you will find some real learning. There you'll get some schooling. There you'll really learn something!"

"The boys are only staying home a week?" the distraught mother gasped, her eyes filling with tears. "The poor boys won't even have a chance to enjoy themselves a little. They won't have a chance to get to know their own home, and I won't be able to get my fill of looking at them!"

"Enough! Enough whining, old woman! Cossacks aren't Cossacks so they can hobnob with women! Given half a chance you'd hide them under your skirt and sit on them like a hen. Off with you, quick, and get the table ready! Lay out everything we have! No need for fritters and poppyseed cakes, or any other delicate little morsels; just bring out some mutton and some goat, and the forty-year-old mead. And some good vodka, none of that fancy liquor with raisins and other little knickknacks in it! I want my vodka so clear and frothing that it hisses and whirls like it's possessed!"

---

* A settlement on the Dnieper in Ukraine, where the Zaporozhian Cossacks had their base camp, the Sech.

Bulba led his sons into the front room. Two pretty maids wearing coin necklaces, who had been busy cleaning, dropped everything and ran. They were evidently frightened by the arrival of the young masters, who never let anyone alone, or else they simply wanted to stick to their girlish ways, squealing and bolting whenever they saw a man, lifting their sleeves to their faces, hiding them in shame. The front room was furnished in the taste of those difficult, warring times, when battles and skirmishes broke out because of the union with Poland. Living traces of those days are found only in the songs and folk epics sung in the Ukraine by old, bearded, blind men quietly strumming their banduras, surrounded by a crowd.* Everything was clean and brightly painted. On the walls hung sabers, whips, bird traps, fishnets, muskets, an intricately carved gunpowder horn, a golden bridle, and a hobble with silver pendants. The windows were small, with round, dim panes such as are now found only in old churches, and through which one could only see if one raised the movable panels. Red drapes hung by the windows and doors. On shelves in the corners stood pots, bottles, flasks of blue and green glass, ornate silver goblets, and gilded cups of every handicraft—Venetian, Turkish, Circassian—that had made their way into Bulba's front room by many paths and through many hands, as was not unusual for those swashbuckling times.† Birch benches ran along the walls in all the rooms. Beneath the icons in the prayer corner stood a massive table, and near it a stove with many ledges and protuberances, surrounded by warm benches. The stove was covered with bright multicolored tiles. All this was very familiar to the two young men, who in the past had walked home every year during the holidays because they did not yet have horses, and because it was not customary to allow students of the Seminary to ride. The only Cossack tradition they had kept was the long forelock, the *chub*, which seasoned Cossacks tugged at in jest.‡ Now that

---

* A bandura is a lutelike instrument used by Ukrainian bards to accompany sung ballads and epics.
† Circassia is a region in the northern Caucasus.
‡ Ukrainian Cossacks shaved their heads, leaving only a forelock, known as *chub*.

they had finished their studies, Bulba had sent them a pair of young stallions from his own herd.

To celebrate his sons' arrival, Bulba called in all the Cossack captains and anyone from his regiment who was within reach. And when his old comrade Captain Dimitro Tovkach came with two officers, Bulba immediately presented his sons to them.

"Here—see what fine boys these are! I'll be sending them to the Sech soon."

The guests congratulated Bulba and the two young men, assuring them that it was a good idea, that there was no better schooling for young men than the Zaporozhian Sech.

"Well, my brothers, seat yourselves at the table wherever you like!" Bulba shouted, and turned to his sons. "First we shall down some vodka! God's blessings upon you, and good health to the two of you! To you, Ostap, and to you, Andri! May God grant that success always follow you in battle, whether you fight heathen, Turk, or Tatar fiend. And if the damn Poles start plotting against our religion, then may you thrash them too! Come, hand me your cup! Good vodka, no? So how does one say 'vodka' in Latin? Ha! Well, my son, those Romans were fools—they didn't even know there was such a thing as vodka! What was that fellow's name again, the one who wrote little Latin ditties? I'm not much of a lettered man, so it's not coming to me right now. Wasn't it Horace, or something?"

"Ha, that's my father for you!" Ostap, the older of the two boys, thought. "There's nothing the old scoundrel doesn't know, and yet he pretends not to."

"It would surprise me if the Archimandrite at the Seminary let you have so much as a whiff of vodka," Taras continued.* "And I trust you were given robust birch-wood and fresh cherry-wood whippings across your backs and your other Cossack parts! And perhaps the cleverer you got the more you got to taste the cat-o'-nine-tails. And

---

* Archimandrite: the head of a Russian Orthodox monastery or group of monasteries.

not only on Saturdays, I'm sure, but on Wednesdays and Thursdays too!"

"There is no reason to remember what was, Papa," Ostap answered coolly. "What was is now past and gone!"

"I'd like to see them try something now!" Andri said. "I'd like to see someone so much as try to touch us. Let some Tatar dog cross my path, and I'll teach him what a Cossack saber is!"

"Well spoken, my son! By God, well spoken indeed! When the time comes I will ride out by your side, by God I will! Why the devil should I sit around here? So I can sow buckwheat? So I can run the household, tend the sheep and pigs, and help the old woman with her sewing and needlework? To the devil with her! I'm a Cossack and will have none of this! So what if there's no war, I'll ride with you to Zaporozhe for some fun, by God I will!"

Old Bulba became increasingly heated, and finally burst into a rage. Then he stood up from the table, composed himself, and stamped his foot.

"We will leave tomorrow! There is no point in dawdling! What enemy can we expect to dig up here? What do we need this house for? What do we need all these pots for?" He began pounding the pots and bottles with his fist and hurling them across the room. His poor wife, used to her husband's outbursts, looked on sadly from where she sat on the bench. She did not dare open her mouth, but when she heard his decision, so dreadful to her, she could not restrain her tears. She looked at her sons, from whom she was in danger of being parted so soon, and no one can describe the mute power of the sadness that trembled in her eyes and on her lips, which were convulsively pressed together.

Bulba was an uncommonly stubborn man. He was a character who could only have sprung forth from the harsh fifteenth century in that half-nomadic corner of Europe, when the whole of primitive Russia's south, abandoned by its princes, was laid waste and left in ruins by the relentless onslaught of the Mongol marauders; it was a time when man, turned out of house and home, became dauntless, when he settled in charred ruins in the face of terrible neighbors and neverending danger, learning to look them in the eye and unlearning that fear exists in the world; when the flames of war gripped the ancient peaceful Slavic spirit, and Cossackry—that wide, raging sweep of Russian character—was introduced, and when the Cossacks, no one knew their number, struck root along the rivers, at crossings, and on embankments. And when the Turkish Sultan asked how many Cossacks there were, he was told, "Who knows! They are scattered over the whole of our steppes. Behind every weed you'll find a Cossack and his steed!" It was truly an extraordinary phenomenon of Russian power, arising from the national heart of fiery poverty. Instead of the former sovereign principalities consisting of small towns of hunters and trappers, instead of minor princes quarreling and trading with these towns, in their place menacing Cossack settlements and strongholds grew, linked by their shared danger and their hatred of the infidel marauders. We know from our history books how the Cossacks' endless skirmishes and restless life saved Europe from the unstoppable infidel attacks that threatened to overthrow her.

The Polish kings who replaced the appanage princes found themselves lords of these wide lands. Far off and weak though they were, these kings understood the importance of the Cossacks and the advantages to be gained from the Cossack life of warring and defending. The Polish kings encouraged and flattered the Cossacks, and under their distant rule the Hetmans, chosen from among the Cossacks themselves, transformed their homesteads and huts into military bastions. Theirs was not a disciplined and organized army—there were none in that era. But in the case of war and a call to arms, within eight days and not a day more every Cossack presented himself in full armor on his horse, receiving only a single gold ducat in payment from the king, and within two weeks an army came together the like of which no recruiting force could have gathered. When the campaign ended, the warriors returned to their meadows and fields by the

Dnieper crossings, fished, traded, brewed beer, and were free Cossacks. Foreigners of the time were astounded by the truly unusual capabilities of the Cossack. There was no craft he was not master of. He could distill vodka, harness a cart, and grind gunpowder; he was adept at blacksmithing and metalwork; and on top of all that, he could feast recklessly, drink, and carouse as only a Russian can.

Besides the registered Cossacks, who felt bound to present themselves in times of war, it was also possible in case of great urgency to gather crowds of eager volunteers. A Cossack captain had only to stroll through a market or across a village square and shout at the top of his voice, "Hey, you beer brewers! Enough of your brewing and lolling around on stove benches and feeding the flies with your fat carcasses! Ride out in quest of a knight's glory and honor! You plowmen, buckwheat sowers, shepherds, and women-chasers! Enough following the plow, sloshing through the mud in your yellow boots, and crawling to women beneath the covers, squandering your knightly strength! It's time to get yourself some Cossack glory!" And these words were like sparks falling onto dry wood. The plowman threw down his plow, the beer brewer pushed over his tubs and smashed his barrels, craftsmen and store owners sent to the devil all their crafts, all their stores, and all the pots in their houses. Anyone and everyone climbed onto his horse. In a word, the Russian character assumed a broad and powerful sweep.

Taras was one of the true old commanders. He was made for the alarms of war, and stood out for the rough straightforwardness of his temper. In those days the influence of Poland had already begun to have an effect on the Russian nobility. Many had adopted Polish customs, flaunting great pomp, keeping astonishing numbers of servants, falcons, huntsmen, feasts, and palaces. Taras did not crave these splendors. He loved the simple life of the Cossack, and quarreled with comrades who were drawn to the Warsaw faction, accusing them of being lackeys of the Polish noblemen. He was eternally restless. He saw himself as the lawful protector of the Russian Orthodox faith. He was quick to enter villages whenever the people complained of oppression by the landlords and the raising of chimney taxes. He and his Cossacks carried out reprisals. Taras lived by the rule that he was always ready to unsheathe his saber in three circumstances: when commissars did not show full respect to Cossack elders, such as not removing their hats in their presence; when anyone made light of the Russian Orthodox faith and ancestral laws; and, needless to say, when faced by heathens or Turks, against whom he felt it was proper to reach for his saber at all times in the name of Christendom.

Now Taras Bulba anticipated with pleasure how he would appear at the Sech with his two sons and say, "Look what splendid fellows I am bringing you!" and how he would present them to all his old, battle-hardened comrades. He saw himself watching the boys' first feats in the military arts and in carousing, which he also considered as one of the foremost knightly virtues. He had originally intended to send his sons to the Sech alone, but their youth and vigor, their strength and physical beauty ignited his warrior's spirit and he decided to go with them himself the very next day, though the only thing arguing for such an action was his obstinate will. He was already rushing about, giving orders, choosing horses and harnesses for his sons, visiting the stables and barns, picking servants who would ride out with them the following day. He left Captain Tovkach in charge, along with the stern order that Tovkach was to appear with the full regiment the instant he sent word from the Sech. Taras Bulba forgot nothing, even though he was still elated and the hops were bubbling through his head. He even ordered that the horses be given water and that the best and hardiest wheat be poured into their mangers. And he returned home tired from all his running around.

"Well, my boys! It's time to get some rest now, and tomorrow we shall tackle whatever God sees fit to send us! No, don't bother fixing our beds! We won't be needing beds—we shall sleep out in the yard!"

Night had barely embraced the sky, but Bulba always went to sleep at an early hour. He lay down on a carpet and covered himself with a sheepskin coat, because the night air was quite chilly and because he liked to sleep as warmly as possible when he was at home. Soon he was snoring, and the whole yard followed suit. All those who were curled up in various corners began snoring and whistling. The first to fall asleep was the watchman, because he had drunk more than anyone else in honor of the young masters' return.

Only the poor mother could not think of sleep. She bent over the pillows of her darling sons, who lay side by side, and combed their young, tousled locks, dampening them with tears. She gazed at them with all her being, with all her feelings. She gazed at them with all her heart and could not look her fill. Her breasts had fed them, she had raised them, cherished them, and now she was to see them but for a moment. "My sons, my darling sons! What will become of you? What fate awaits you?" she whispered, her tears stopping in the wrinkles that had transformed her once-beautiful face. She was in fact a sad figure, like all women of that distant century. She had only lived love for an instant, in the first flames of passion, the first flames of youth—and already her stern seducer turned away from her in favor of his sword, his comrades, and their carousing. One year she would see her husband for two or three days, and then many years would pass in which she neither heard nor saw anything of him. And even when she saw him, when they lived together, what kind of life was that? She had to bear his insults and beatings. The only caresses she knew were dealt her as alms; she was like a strange being among this medley of womanless knights upon whom dissipated Zaporozhe had cast its grim shadow. Her bleak youth had flashed past; her beautiful fresh cheeks and breasts, prematurely covered with wrinkles, had withered unkissed. All her love and feeling, all that is tender and passionate in woman, turned into maternal love. With fire, passion, and tears she hovered over her children like a gull. Her sons, her beloved sons, were now being taken away from her, taken away, and she would never see them again! Who knew, perhaps a Tatar would slice off their heads the first time they rode into battle, and she would never know where their bodies were thrown, their flesh pecked at by roadside birds of prey. She was ready to sacrifice all she had for each drop of their blood. Sobbing, she gazed into their eyes, which all-powerful sleep was beginning to close, and thought, "Perhaps when Bulba wakes up he might put off their leaving for a day or two. Perhaps it was just the drink that made him think of leaving so early."

From the heights of the sky the moon illuminated the whole courtyard filled with sleeping men and the thick clumps of pussy willow and tall steppe grass that engulfed the paling around the yard. She sat by the heads of her sweet sons without taking her eyes from them for even an instant and without thinking of sleep. The horses, sensing the approach of dawn, had stopped grazing and lay down on the grass. The upper leaves of the pussy willows began to whisper, and gradually the whispering began to descend. She sat there until daybreak, not in the least tired, wishing deep inside that the night would last much longer. The gentle neighing of a foal sounded from the steppes. Strips of red stretched across the sky.

Bulba suddenly awoke and jumped to his feet. He remembered everything he had ordered done the night before.

"Well, my boys, you've had your share of sleep! Come on, it's time to get going! Water the horses! Where's the old woman?" (That was how he usually referred to his wife.) "Get a move on, old woman! Fix us something to eat—we have a long road ahead of us!"

The poor old woman, robbed of her last hopes, dragged herself dejectedly into the hut. Weeping, she busied herself preparing breakfast while Bulba shouted orders and headed to the stables to choose the best bridles for his sons' horses. The young Seminary students had undergone quite a transformation. Instead of their old, bespattered boots, they were now wearing new red ones of morocco leather reinforced with silver studs, and their trousers, wide as the Black Sea, with a thousand folds and pleats, were belted with a golden sash from which hung a long strap with tassels and other trinkets and to which their gunpowder horns were tied. Their scarlet Cossack jackets, the cloth bright as fire, were girded with ornate belts in which richly carved Turkish pistols were stuck. Their sabers swung against their legs. Their faces, little burnt by the sun, seemed handsomer and whiter, and their young black mustaches somehow underlined the paleness of the healthy, robust color of their youth. Their faces were striking beneath their tall, black, golden-topped lambskin hats. Their poor mother! She looked at them and could not utter a word, her tears trapped within her eyes.

"Well, my sons, everything is ready! There's no point lingering!" Bulba finally pronounced. "Now, as Christian custom has it, we must all sit together one last time before we leave."

And they all sat down together, even the lackeys who had been standing reverently by the doors.

"Lay a blessing upon your children, Mother!" Bulba told his wife. "Pray to God that they fight with valor, that they will always defend their knightly honor, and that they will always fight for the True Faith—for if they do not, it would be better for them not to walk the earth! Go to your mother, my sons: a mother's prayer can save a man both on water and on land."

Their weak and sobbing mother embraced them as only a mother can, and hung two small icons around their necks.

"May the Mother of God ... protect you ... and do not forget your own mother, my darling sons ... send word to me that you are well...." She was not able to speak further.

"Let's go, my boys!" Bulba shouted.

The saddled horses stood in front of the door. Bulba jumped onto Devil, who suddenly veered to the side, feeling the twenty-*pood* load on his back, for Bulba was uncommonly stout and brawny.*

When the mother saw that her sons were already mounted, she rushed forward to the younger, whose features still retained a kind of tenderness. She grabbed the stirrup, and clung to his saddle with des-

---

* The *pood* is a Russian unit of weight equal to approximately thirty-six pounds.

peration in her eyes. Two burly Cossacks carefully pulled her away and carried her into the house. But as they rode out of the gate she came rushing out with the lightness of a wild goat, unimaginable at her age, held one of the horses with incomprehensible strength, and embraced her son with blind, crazed fervor. She was again carried into the house.

The young Cossacks rode off sadly, holding back their tears out of fear of their father, who was perturbed himself, although he struggled not to show it. It was a gray day. The green steppes glittered brightly. Birds chattered discordantly. After they had ridden awhile they looked back. It was as if their homestead had sunk into the steppes. All that could be seen above the grass were the two chimneys of their modest house and the tops of the trees, on the branches of which they had once climbed like squirrels. All they saw before them now, stretching out into the endless distance, was the steppe, calling to their minds the whole story of their lives, from the years when they had rolled about in the dew-wet grass to the years when they lay in wait for black-browed Cossack maidens who bolted over these steppes on fresh and nimble legs. Now only the pole above the well, with a cartwheel fastened to its top, jutted into the sky. Already the plain across which they had ridden seemed like a mountain that hides everything from view. Farewell to childhood, to games, to everything, everything!

2

The three horsemen rode on in silence. Old Taras was thinking of the past: he saw his youth before him, the years that had flowed by, the years that every Cossack mourns, wishing that he had the strength of youth throughout his life. He was wondering which of his old comrades in arms he would see at the Sech. He counted up those who had already passed away and those who were still alive. A tear slowly formed in his eye, and his graying head sank despondently.

His sons were immersed in other thoughts. But more needs to be said about these sons. At twelve, they had been sent to the Kiev Seminary because all the prominent men of the time thought it vital that their sons be provided with an education, even if everything they learned was later forgotten. When the boys entered the Seminary they were wild, like all the other new pupils who had been raised in the open. At the Seminary they were given a light veneer that made them all resemble one another. Ostap, the older of the two, ran away in the first year. He was brought back, given a terrible beating, and forced to return to his books. Four times he took his primer and buried it on the

Seminary grounds, and four times, after an inhuman beating, he was given a new one. He would have doubtless buried the fifth primer, too, had his father not sworn a solemn oath that he would have him locked up for twenty years as a novice in a monastery, and also sworn that Ostap would never see Zaporozhe if he did not learn everything the Seminary had to teach. It was interesting that these were the words of Taras Bulba, who always cursed learning and, as we have already seen, advised his sons not to concern themselves with it at all.

After Bulba's oath, Ostap had begun applying himself to the tedious books with uncommon diligence, and soon was counted among the best pupils. The academic curriculum of that era was very much at odds with the way of life, and the curriculum's scholastic, grammatical, rhetorical, and logical divisions in no way corresponded to the needs of the times. Even if what the pupils were taught had been less scholarly, they could never hope to apply it. In those days, the most learned men were also the most ignorant, far removed from experience. Not to mention that the republican setup of the Seminary and the multitude of young, robust, healthy boys could not but inspire activities that had nothing to do with the curriculum. It might have been the harsh conditions, or the frequent punishment fasts, or the many needs stirred up in the strong and healthy youths, that kindled in them the kind of enterprise they later developed in Zaporozhe. When the famished students roamed the streets of Kiev, all the townsfolk were on guard. The moment the women of the bazaars saw a student walk by, they quickly covered their pies, bread rolls, and pumpkin seeds the way female eagles will cover their young. The head student, obliged by his status to see to the welfare of his peers, had such capacious pockets in his trousers that he could empty a gaping market woman's entire stall into them.

The students were a world unto themselves. They were not admitted into the higher circles of the Polish and Russian nobility. The governor, Adam Kisel, notwithstanding his patronage of the academy, was far from introducing the students into society. Indeed, he had issued

orders that they be held in stricter check—orders that were quite un-
necessary, as the Seminary's rector and monks were anything but spar-
ing with the rod and whip, and had the lictors give the pupils such
lashings that weeks afterward they were still rubbing the seats of their
pants. For many of the boys, the beatings seemed but a little sharper
than good pepper vodka; and yet there were also boys who abhorred
the perpetual thrashings and ran away to Zaporozhe, provided they
could find the way there and were not caught.

Ostap Bulba began studying logic and even theology with great
application, and yet he still did not manage to escape the relentless
whip. Inevitably, this hardened his character and lent him the kind of
toughness that sets a Cossack apart. Ostap was considered the best
comrade one could have. He rarely led his peers in wayward undertakings, such as the plundering of gardens or orchards, and was always
one of the first to appear under the flag of an enterprising student.
Never in any circumstances would he betray a comrade. No rod or
whip could induce him to do that. He stood firm in the face of all
temptations except those of war and wild carousing. He barely ever
thought of anything else. He was forthright with his peers. He had a
goodness of the kind that could only exist in that era in a character
like his. He was deeply moved by his poor mother's tears, and it was
they and they alone that saddened him and made him hang his head in
thought.

His younger brother Andri's feelings were somewhat livelier, and in
a sense more developed. He had studied with more gusto, and without
having to force himself. He was also more resourceful than his brother.
He led his peers more frequently in dangerous undertakings, and at
times managed to dodge punishment with great ingenuity, while his
brother Ostap readily took off his shirt and lay down on the floor to be
flogged, refusing to ask for mercy. Andri thirsted for heroic feats, but
his soul was also open to other feelings. When he reached his eigh-
teenth year, the need for love flared up within him. Fiery images of a

woman appeared ever more often in his dreams. As he listened to philosophical debates, he saw her constantly, fresh, dark-eyed, and tender. Her luminous taut breasts and her wonderful, soft arms, completely bare, sparkled perpetually before him. Even her dress, sweeping over her virginal but powerful limbs, exuded an inexpressible voluptuousness. He carefully hid the stirrings of his youthful passionate soul from his comrades, because in those days it was shameful and dishonorable for a Cossack to think about women and love before he knew battle. In the last few years, Andri had rarely led a pack of students on escapades, but now roamed alone through the more remote streets of Kiev, past cherry orchards and low houses that peered beckoningly into the street. Sometimes he even ended up on the boulevards of the aristocrats in what is today Kiev's old town, where Ukrainian and Polish noblemen lived and where the houses were stylish. Once, as he stood gaping on one of these boulevards, he was almost run over by the large carriage of a Polish nobleman, and the coachman, who had a frightening mustache, gave him a sharp lash with his whip. Andri flared up and with crazed audacity grabbed the rear wheel with his powerful hand, bringing the carriage to a halt. The coachman, fearing a scuffle, whipped the horses into a gallop, and Andri, who fortunately managed to pull his hand away from the spokes, went tumbling to the ground with his face in the mud.

A ringing, harmonious laugh came from somewhere above him. He raised his eyes and saw the most beautiful girl he had ever seen, standing at a window. She was dark-eyed and white as snow lit by the rosy morning sun. She laughed with all her heart, and her laughter lent a sparkling strength to her dazzling beauty. Andri was struck dumb. He stared at her, absently wiping the dirt from his face, smudging it even more. Who could this beauty be? He asked the group of servants in rich livery who were standing around a young bandura player by the gate. But the servants guffawed when they saw his mud-smeared face and did not deign to give him an answer. He finally discovered that she was the daughter of the governor of Kovno, who was currently visiting Kiev.

The following night, with all the audacity of a Seminary student, he slipped through the fence into the garden, climbed a tree, the branches of which stretched over the house, and from the tree crept out onto the roof and lowered himself through a chimney into the bedroom of the beautiful girl, who was sitting by a candle taking off her precious earrings. The Polish beauty was so startled at suddenly seeing an unknown man before her that she was unable to utter a single word. But she quickly saw that he stood there timidly with lowered eyes, not daring to move a finger. She recognized him as the boy she had seen fall in the street, and she was again gripped by laughter. There was nothing frightening in Andri's features—he was, in fact, a very handsome fellow. She laughed out loud, and began toying with him. She was frivolous, as all Polish girls are, but her eyes, her wonderful, penetratingly bright eyes, cast lingering glances. He could not stir, and felt as if he had been bound and gagged. The governor's daughter boldly came over to him, placed her sparkling diadem on his head, clipped her earrings on his lips, and slipped onto him her maidenly, flimsy blouse with its frills and gold embroidery. She adorned him and did a thousand different foolish things with him in the overfamiliar, childish way characteristic of Polish girls, perplexing the poor student even more. He was a funny sight, his mouth hanging open as he stared into her dazzling eyes.

A sudden knock at the door startled her, and she quickly made Andri hide under the bed. But the moment the danger was past she told her maid, an indentured Tatar woman, to cautiously take Andri down to the garden and see to it that he slipped back out through the fence. But this time Andri was not as successful. The watchman woke up and grabbed hold of his legs, and servants came running and beat him as he ran out into the street. His fast legs saved him.

It was now dangerous for Andri to walk past the house, because the governor had many servants. Andri met her again in church. She noticed him and smiled at him pleasantly, as at an old acquaintance. He caught a glimpse of her one other time, but then the governor of Kovno left and, instead of the beautiful dark-eyed Polish girl, Andri saw a fat face peering out the window. This is what Andri was thinking of as they rode over the steppe, his head hanging and his eyes fixed on his horse's mane.

By now the steppe had enfolded the Cossacks in its green embrace, and the high grass surrounding them covered them, so that only their black lambskin hats flashed above it.

"Hey, hey, hey! Why are you boys suddenly so quiet?" Bulba shouted, shaking himself out of his brooding state. "You're like a pair of monks! To the devil with your somber thoughts! Let's smoke a pipe before we spur the horses and fly so fast that even birds cannot keep up with us!"

The Cossacks leaned forward over their horses and disappeared into the grass. Now not even their black hats could be seen. Only the stream of parting grass showed the track of their fast gallop.

For some time the sun had been peering from the now cloudless sky, and was bathing the steppe in its bracing, warming light. Everything that was troubled and pensive in the Cossacks' souls dispersed in an instant, and their hearts soared like birds.

The farther they rode into the steppe, the more beautiful it became. In those days the whole south, the vast expanse of what today is Novorossiya, all the way down to the Black Sea, was a green virgin wilderness. No plow had ever cut the boundless waves of wild grasses, and only the hooves of the horses hidden within the steppe as in a forest had trampled the earth. Here was the best that nature had to offer. The whole land was a gold-green ocean over which a million flowers had been scattered. Blue, purple, and lilac cornflowers shimmered through the thin, tall grass, above which yellow brushweeds stuck their pyramidal tips. White clover with umbrella-like hats sparkled over the surface. Succulent ears of wheat, sprouted from God knows what seed, thrived in the thicket. Partridges darted with craning necks among spindly roots. The air was filled with a thousand different birdcalls. Hawks hung motionless in the sky, their wings spread wide and their eyes fixed on the grass. The call of a moving cloud of wild geese resounded from a distant lake. A gull rose from the grass with an even flutter, and bathed luxuriantly in the blue waves of the air. The gull disappeared high in the sky, shimmering only as a dot. Suddenly it raised its wings and shone before the sun. Accursed steppes, how beautiful you are!

Our travelers stopped for only a few minutes to eat. Their retinue of ten Cossacks dismounted and unfastened the wooden flasks of vodka and the gourds that served as cups. They ate bread and rolls with lard, drank a cupful of vodka—but only for strength, since Taras Bulba did not permit drunkenness on a journey—and then rode on until evening.

At dusk the whole steppe changed. Its bright and colorful expanse was gripped by a last blazing gleam of sunlight, and one could see it gradually fade, a spreading shadow turning it a somber green. The vapors rose more densely—every little blossom, every blade of grass, exuded an aroma, the whole steppe smoldering in fragrance. The sky, black as ink, looked as if a gigantic brush had spread wide strips of rosy gold over it. Here and there, airy, transparent clouds shimmered in little white clumps, and the freshest breeze, seductive as ocean waves, barely swayed over the tips of the grass, brushing against the riders' cheeks. All the music that had sounded during the day fell silent, and then changed into another music. Colorful ground squirrels popped out of their burrows, stood on their hind legs, and filled the steppe with their whistling. The chirping of the grasshoppers grew stronger. At times a swan's call echoed like silver through the air from a remote lake.

The travelers stopped and made camp for the night. They lit a fire and placed a kettle over it, in which they boiled some wheat kasha.

Steam began rising crookedly through the air. The Cossacks ate and then lay down to sleep on their tunics, leaving their horses tethered nearby in the grass. The night stars gazed straight down at them. In their ears echoed the boundless insect world that filled the grass with chirping, whistling, and chirring. All this resounded through the night, cleansed in the fresh air and lulling the dozing ear. Had any of the Cossacks risen to gaze at the steppe, they would have seen it sown with the glittering sparks of fireflies. At times, parts of the night sky were lit by the distant glow of dry reeds burning in meadows and along riverbanks, and a dark line of swans flying north was suddenly illuminated in the fire's rosy-silver light, as if shreds of red cloth were flying through the dark sky.

The journey continued without incident. Nowhere did the travelers come across trees; it was always the same endless, free, beautiful steppe. Rarely did they see the faraway treetops of a distant forest stretching along the banks of the Dnieper. Only once did Taras point out a small, blackish spot in the distant grass and say, "See that, my boys? That's a galloping Tatar!" And a small, mustached face peered at them from a distance with its slanted eyes, sniffed at the air like a hunting dog, and, realizing that the Cossacks numbered thirteen, bolted like a stag.

"Well, my boys! Try catching that Tatar! Or rather don't try—you'll never catch him! His horse is even faster than mine!"

And yet Bulba took precautions, fearing an ambush. They galloped to the Tatarka, a small river that emptied into the Dnieper, hurled themselves with their horses into the water, and floated quite a long way downstream in order to hide their trail before they climbed back up the riverbank to continue their journey.

Within three days they were approaching their goal. The air had suddenly grown cooler. They felt the closeness of the Dnieper. It gleamed in the distance; its dark ribbon stood out against the horizon and fanned them with its cold waves, gradually spreading out as they rode on and finally engulfing half the surface of the land. This was the place where the Dnieper, hitherto locked in its banks, finally triumphed and broke free, roaring like the sea, the islands that had been hurled into its center pressing its waters even further out of its banks, its waves spreading wide over the earth, meeting neither rock nor mound. The Cossacks dismounted and climbed onto a ferry, and after a three-hour passage reached the shores of Khortitsa Island, where the Sech, which moved so often, was located in those days.

Onshore, a crowd of people was arguing with the ferrymen. The Cossacks rebridled their horses, and Taras assumed a dignified air, tightened his belt, and proudly ran his fingers over his mustache. His sons also eyed each other from head to foot with a mixture of apprehension and indefinable pleasure, and the whole company rode off to the settlement that lay about half a verst from the Sech.* They were deafened by fifty blacksmith hammers pounding in twenty-five smithies dug into the earth and covered with turf. Strong tanners sat outside under canopies, kneading bull hides with their powerful fingers. Peddlers sat behind piles of flint, tinder, and powder. An Armenian was hanging expensive shawls. A Tatar was roasting mutton with dough on a spit. A Jew, his head craning forward, was tapping vodka from a barrel. But the first man they came across was a Zaporozhian Cossack. He was lying asleep in the middle of the road, his arms and legs spread out. Taras Bulba could not refrain from stopping and admiring him.

"Look how splendid he is, stretched out! I'll be damned, but he makes a fine figure!" he said, stopping the horses.

And it was a very bold picture indeed: the Cossack lay stretched out on the street like a lion. His long forelock lay a good foot across the dirt. His wide trousers, made of precious crimson material, were tar-spattered to show how little he cared for them. Bulba stood admiring him awhile and then rode on along the narrow street. It was cluttered

---

* Verst: a distance equivalent to about two thirds of a mile.

with workshops going about their daily business, and bustling with people of all nations. This settlement, reminiscent of a fair, dressed and fed the Sech, which knew only how to carouse and fire weapons.

Finally they passed the settlement and saw a few scattered huts, some covered with turf, some with felt in Tatar fashion. Cannons stood on some of the roofs. Here there were no fences to be seen, nor the kind of awninged huts on little stilts that filled the settlement. There was a small rampart and a wooden barricade that stood completely unguarded, testifying to a terrible indifference. A few robust Zaporozhian Cossacks, who were lying about in the middle of the road with tobacco pipes in their mouths, looked at the travelers without interest and did not move. Taras and his sons rode carefully among them, calling out "Greetings, brothers!"

"Greetings to you!" the Zaporozhians called back.

The whole field was filled with a colorful tangle of Cossacks. By their weather-beaten faces it was clear that these men had been forged in battle, having tasted every adversity. So this was the Sech! This was the source from which surged all those proud men, strong as lions! From here freedom and Cossackry had spilled over the whole Ukraine!

The travelers rode out onto a vast square on which the council usually gathered. A bare-chested Zaporozhian was sitting on a large overturned keg. He had his shirt in his hands and was slowly darning it. The travelers' path was blocked again, this time by a large crowd of musicians, in the midst of whom danced a young Zaporozhian, throwing his arms into the air, his hat at a jaunty angle.

"Musicians, more life!" he shouted. "Foma, don't begrudge honest Christian men some vodka!" And Foma, who had a black eye, poured large mugs of vodka free of charge to everyone around. Next to the young dancing Cossack, four old men were executing fast, delicate footwork, their legs flying up like whirlwinds, almost hitting the heads of the musicians, then suddenly plunging down. The old men crouched and began pummeling the earth with their silver-studded boots. The earth droned dully all around, and the air far and wide was filled with hopaks and tropaks pounded out by their hammering soles.* One man was yelling louder than the rest as he flew at the heels of the others in the dance. His Cossack forelock swung in the air, and his powerful chest was bare under the heavy winter sheepskin coat slung over his shoulders. Sweat was pouring from him.

"At least take off that coat!" Taras shouted. "It's steaming already!"

"I can't!" the Cossack shouted back.

"Why not?"

"I can't! Anything I take off, I sell for liquor!"

The fellow was no longer wearing a hat, nor did he have a belt for his caftan, nor an embroidered handkerchief—he'd sold everything to the devil.

The crowd grew. The dancing men were joined by others, and it was a delight to see how this freest and wildest of dances, called the kazachok after the robust Cossacks who had invented it, dragged with it everything in its path.

"If I wasn't in my saddle," Taras called out, "I'd be down there myself dancing!"

Old and gray Cossack forelocks began appearing among the crowd, men revered for their years of service to the Sech, among them even some Cossack elders. Taras soon encountered many faces he knew. Ostap and Andri heard a string of greetings.

"That's you, is it, Pecheritsa? Greetings, Kosolup!"

"Taras! Where have you ridden in from?"

"How is it you are here, Doloto?"

"Greetings, Kirdyaga! Hello there, Gusti! Well! To see you here, Remen!"

The heroes, who had gathered from the whole riotous world of eastern Russia, kissed each other, and one question unleashed another.

---

* The hopak and tropak are traditional Ukrainian dances.

"And where's Kasan? What about Borodavka? And Koloper? And what about Pidsishok?"

Taras Bulba was told that Borodavka had been hanged in Tolopan, that Koloper had been skinned alive at Kisikirmen, and that Pidsishok's head had been salted in a barrel and sent all the way to Czargrad.* Old Bulba hung his head.

"They were good Cossacks!" he said solemnly.

---

* The old Russian name for Constantinople.

3

Taras Bulba and his sons had now been almost a week at the Sech.
Ostap and Andri did not busy themselves much with military
training—the Sech did not trouble itself with such things, thinking
them a waste of time. Its young warriors were formed only one way:
in the blaze of battle, which for this reason was almost endless. During the brief periods between battles, the Cossacks felt that training
was tiresome, except for a little target practice and a few horse races
and hunting expeditions into the steppe. The rest of the time was
spent carousing, a sign of the raging sweep of the Cossacks' free spirit.
The whole Sech presented an unusual sight. It was a kind of uninter-
rupted feast that began noisily and had no end. Some of the Cossacks
did busy themselves with handicrafts, or kept stalls and traded, but
most caroused from morning to night as long as coins jingled in their
pockets and the spoils of war had not yet passed into the hands of the
traders and tavern keepers. This out-and-out feasting had something
bewitching about it. The revelers were not drinking away their trou-
bles, but were on a crazed and exuberant spree. A man who came to

the Sech cast off all that had preoccupied him. He spat, as one might say, on his past, and gave himself over to freedom and the camaraderie of his peers, who like him were revelers without family and with no other home than the open sky and the eternal carousing soul. This gave rise to a crazed merriment that could not have sprung from any other source.

The tales and yarns heard among the crowds of Cossacks lolling lazily on the ground were often so funny, and breathed such a power of life, that one had to have the cool blood of a Zaporozhian Cossack to keep a straight face, with mustaches not perturbed by a single twitch—a trait which to this day distinguishes the southern Russian. The carousing was boisterous, yet not the kind one finds in dark taverns, where a man seeks to forget himself in somber cheer. The Cossacks made the tight kind of circle one finds among pupils in a schoolhouse. The only difference was that here, instead of being fed the alphabet and the schoolmaster's dreary explanations, they rode out in sorties on five thousand horses; instead of a meadow where pupils might play ball, they roamed over dangerous borderlands where the Tatar raised his nimble head and the green-turbaned Turk peered impassively. Instead of the subjugation that united pupils in a school, the Cossacks turned their backs on their fathers and mothers of their own free will, and abandoned their homes. There were men here who had barely escaped the hangman's noose, who instead of bleak death saw life, and a very boisterous and riotous life at that. There were those who, like aristocrats, could not keep a single brass coin in their pockets, and those who would have thought such a coin a fortune, but who, thanks to the Jewish moneylenders, had pockets you could turn inside out without the slightest fear of anything dropping out. Here, too, were all the escaped Seminary students who were no longer able to bear the academy's rod and who had left without an iota of learning. But alongside them were also those who knew of Horace, Cicero, and the Roman Republic. The Sech harbored many officers who would later make a name for themselves in the Imperial Army.

There was a great number of educated and experienced partisans who cherished the noble belief that it was of little consequence where one fought, as long as one did fight, for it was unseemly for a man of mettle not to be in battle. There were also many who came to the Sech merely to be able to say that they had been there and were thus hardened knights. This strange republic was a necessity in that era. Lovers of a life of war, of golden chalices, rich brocade, gold ducats, and silver reals could always find what they were seeking. Only admirers of women would find nothing, for there was not a single woman, even in the settlement around the Sech.

Ostap and Andri found it extremely odd that hordes of men simply wandered into the Sech without anyone questioning who they were, where they came from, or what their names might be. These men came as if they were returning home after an hour's absence, and went over to see the Ataman.*

"Greetings! So, you believe in Christ?" the Ataman would ask.

"I do!"

"How about the Holy Trinity?"

"I do!"

"You go to church?"

"I do!"

"So let's see you cross yourself!"

The new arrival would cross himself.

"Well then," the Ataman would say, "go join one of the companies."

And that was the end of the initiation ceremony. The whole Sech was of one faith and prepared to defend this faith to the last drop of blood, though it disregarded all fasting periods and temperance. Only extremely covetous Jews, Armenians, and Tatars dared live and trade in the settlement, for the Zaporozhians never liked trading, and always paid with fistfuls of money. And yet the lot of these covetous traders

---

* A Cossack leader.

was pitiful. They called to mind the people who lived at the foot of Mount Vesuvius, because the moment the swashbuckling Zaporozhians ran out of money they ransacked the stores and took whatever they wanted without paying.

The Sech was made up of some sixty companies, which resembled separate, independent republics, and resembled even more a school or academy where students are given full board. No one acquired or owned anything at all. The company captain kept everything in his hands, and for that reason was usually called Papa. He kept the money, clothes, and all the provisions: flour paste, kasha, and even fuel. Often disputes broke out among the companies. When that happened, everyone came to blows. The companies poured out over the square, and there was a big brawl until one side finally got the better of the other, at which point they would all begin carousing. This was the Sech, so attractive to the young men.

Ostap and Andri threw themselves into this sea of revelry with all the fervor of youth and embraced their new life, forgetting their home, the Seminary, and everything that had troubled their souls. They were fascinated by the wild ways of the Sech and the rough code of justice, which at times struck them as too harsh in such a willful republic. If a Cossack was caught stealing, stole even a trifle, it was viewed as an affront to the whole of Cossackry. Stripped of all honor, he would be tied to a post of shame with a cudgel placed next to him, and every passerby was required to strike him until he had been bludgeoned to death. A Cossack who defaulted on his debts was chained to a cannon and had to sit there until one of his comrades paid the debt. But what struck Andri most was the terrible penalty for murder. A pit was dug and the murderer, still alive, was lowered into it. The coffin of the victim was placed over him, after which the grave was covered with earth. For a long time afterward, Andri could not banish the awful execution rite from his mind, and kept imagining the man buried alive with the terrible coffin.

Soon the two young men were in good standing with all the Cossacks. They often rode out into the steppe with comrades to shoot the boundless variety of birds, deer, and goats, or rode out to the lakes, rivers, and streams, which were assigned to each company by lot. There they cast nets and pulled in plentiful catches for the whole company. Though no one in the Sech practiced the war skills that a Cossack needs, Ostap and Andri stood out among the other young men through their daring and success. They shot at targets with great accuracy, and swam the Dnieper against the current, a feat for which novices were festively inducted into Cossack ranks.

But old Taras was preparing something different for them. This life of idleness went against his grain. He kept wondering how he might rouse the Sech to some valiant enterprise, where the Cossacks could then carouse as befits knights. Finally one day he went over to the Ataman.

"Isn't it time these Zaporozhians had some fun?" he asked him gruffly.

"There's no fun to be had," the Ataman answered, pulling out of his mouth the pipe he was smoking, and spitting to the side.

"What do you mean, no fun to be had? We could go after the Turk or the Tatar."

"We can't go after the Turk or the Tatar."

"What do you mean we can't go after them?"

"We promised the Sultan peace."

"But he's a heathen, and God and Holy Writ demand that we kill heathens!"

"We don't have the right. It was by our faith that we swore peace; otherwise we could have gone after them. But as things stand, we can't."

"What do you mean we can't? Why are you saying we don't have the right? I have two sons here, both of them young men! Not once has either of them seen battle, and you're telling me we don't have the right, and that the Zaporozhians need not go to war?"

"They must not go to war."

"Then Cossack strength will be wasted! The men will go to the dogs without a good cause to fight for, and our Cossacks will be of use neither to our fatherland nor to the Christian world! Then tell me what we are living for! You are a clever man, we didn't elect you Ataman for nothing, so can you tell me what we are living for?"

The Ataman did not respond to this question. He was a stubborn Cossack. He remained silent for a while and then said, "Be that as it may, there will be no war."

"There will be no war?" Taras asked once more.

"No, there won't."

"You are saying there is not the slightest chance?"

"No, there's not the slightest chance."

"Just you wait, you devil!" Bulba thought. "You haven't heard the last of this!" And he swore then and there that he would seek revenge on the Ataman.

Taras spoke to some of the men and threw a feast for them; the drunken Cossacks, few in number, went rushing straight to the square where the drums were beaten to call together an assembly. Not finding the drumstick, which was always kept by the drummer, the Cossacks grabbed bits of wood and began beating the drums. The first man to come running was the drummer, a tall man with only one eye, which was nevertheless very heavy with sleep.

"Who dared do this?" he shouted.

"Hold your tongue and pound the drum! That's an order!" the carousing men shouted back.

The drummer took out the drumsticks he had brought, because he well knew the outcome of such matters. The drums thundered, and soon black clusters of Cossacks began gathering on the square like bees. They formed a circle, and after the third drumroll the council of commanders appeared: the Ataman with his staff in his hand—a sign of his dignity—the judge carrying the war crest, the scribe with his inkpot, and the captain with his baton. The Ataman and the council commanders took off their hats and bowed in all directions to the Cossacks, who stood glaring at them haughtily, their arms on their hips.

"What is the meaning of this gathering? What is it you want?" the Ataman asked.

His voice was drowned out by shouts and curses.

"Lay down your staff!" shouted Cossacks from the crowd. "Lay it down, you devil! Lay it down immediately! We don't want you anymore!"

Some of the sober companies seemed to want to resist, and soon different groups, drunk and sober, flew at each other with their fists. The noise and shouting spread through the crowd.

The Ataman wanted to speak but, sensing that the heated, self-willed crowd would beat him to death, which almost always happened on similar occasions, he bent his head down low, put on his hat, and hid in the crowd.

"Brothers, are you also ordering us to lay down our regalia?" shouted the judge, the scribe, and the captain, ready to relinquish the crest, the inkpot, and the baton.

"Stay where you are!" the crowd shouted. "We only want to get rid of the Ataman, because he is an old woman! What we need is a real Ataman!"

"Who will you elect as Ataman?" the commanders asked.

"Kukubenko!" some of the Cossacks shouted.

"No, we don't want Kukubenko!" others yelled. "He's not up to it, he's still got his mother's milk on his lips!"

"We want Shilo!" others shouted. "Make Shilo the Ataman!"

"To hell with Shilo!" others shouted back. "What kind of Cossack is he? We caught him stealing like a low Tatar, the son of a bitch! He should be put in a sack and drowned, the drunken bastard!"

"Borodaty! We want Borodaty!"

"No we don't! To hell with the bastard!"

"Call out Kirdyaga's name," Taras Bulba whispered to some of the men.

"Kirdyaga! Kirdyaga!" the crowd began to shout.

"Borodaty! Borodaty!"

"Kirdyaga! Kirdyaga!"

"Shilo!"

"Damn Shilo! We want Kirdyaga!"

On hearing their names shouted, the candidates quickly left the crowd so that no one would think they were trying to further their own cause.

Kirdyaga's name was shouted louder than all the rest.

"Borodaty!"

Different factions furthered their candidates' names with their fists, and Kirdyaga triumphed.

"Go get Kirdyaga!" the Zaporozhians shouted.

A dozen or so Cossacks staggered out of the crowd, some so drunk they were barely able to stand, and went looking for Kirdyaga to tell him he had been chosen Ataman.

Kirdyaga, a clever Cossack advanced in years, was sitting in his hut as if unaware of what had occurred.

"Yes, brothers? What do you want?" he asked.

"Come with us! You have been elected Ataman!"

"Upon my soul! I do not deserve such an honor!" Kirdyaga exclaimed. "How can I be the Ataman, I'm not wise enough to undertake such an office. In all the army, couldn't you have found someone better?"

"You are to come with us!" the Zaporozhians shouted. Two of them grabbed him by the arms, and though he dug in his heels he was dragged to the square with swearing, blows, kicks, and admonishments. "Stop dragging your feet, you devil! You should accept the honor we gave you, you dog!"

Kirdyaga was brought before the Cossack assembly.

"Well, brothers," the Cossacks accompanying him called out, "is everyone agreed that this man is to be our Ataman?"

"We agree!" the crowd shouted, and the whole square thundered with their yells.

One of the council commanders took the staff and brought it to the newly elected Ataman. Kirdyaga declined the staff, as custom dictated. The elder held it out to him a second time. Kirdyaga refused it again, but then the third time accepted it. Shouts of approval resounded through the crowd, and once more the whole field rumbled with the Cossacks' voices. Four of the oldest gray-bearded and gray-forelocked Cossacks stepped out of the crowd (there were no very old men at the Sech, as Zaporozhians never died of old age); each picked up a clump of earth muddied by a downpour earlier in the day and placed it on Kirdyaga's head. The wet earth trickled over his mustache and cheeks, smudging his whole face. Kirdyaga stood motionless, and thanked the Cossacks for the honor they had accorded him.

This was how the noisy assembly ended, and in all likelihood no man was happier than Bulba. He had managed to avenge himself on the previous Ataman, and furthermore Kirdyaga had been his comrade-in-arms. They had fought side by side in many battles both on land and sea and shared all the hardships of a life of war.

The crowd immediately dispersed and started celebrating the election, and soon revelries began the like of which Ostap and Andri had never seen. Stores were ransacked of mead, vodka, and beer, and the storekeepers were glad to escape with their lives. The whole night passed with shouting and songs glorifying past battles. The rising moon saw crowds of musicians walking the streets with banduras, horns, and round balalaikas, and singers who were kept at the Sech for church choirs and to sing of the glorious deeds of the Zaporozhians.

Finally the Cossacks' powerful heads began drooping in drunkenness and fatigue, and here and there men began falling to the ground. Comrades hugged each other, deeply moved and even in tears, as they tumbled over together. A throng of Cossacks lay in a heap. One man, trying to figure out how to lie down most comfortably, settled down in a wooden trough. The last man standing made some rambling speeches. Finally he too succumbed to drunkenness and tumbled to the ground. The whole Sech was asleep.

4

The very next day, Taras Bulba went to consult with the new Ataman about how to rouse the Cossacks into action. The new Ataman was a clever, crafty man who knew the Zaporozhians inside out. "We cannot break the oath we took. We simply cannot do that!" he said, but after a few moments of silence added, "And yet I'm sure something can be done. We mustn't actually break our oath, yet there must be a way. Let's have all the men gather together, but as if they are gathering of their own free will and not by my order. I am sure you know how to manage that. Then the council commanders and I will come out on the square as if we had no idea what was happening."

Within the hour the drumroll began. Drunken, besotted Zaporozhians appeared. A million Cossack hats came streaming into the square. Voices arose from all sides:

"Who?"

"What?"

"Why has a meeting been called?"

But nobody answered.

Then other voices were heard:

"Our Cossack strength is going to waste, for there is no war!"

"Our commanders are turning into slugs, their faces bloated with fat!"

"Is there justice in this world?"

More and more voices shouted, "No, there is no justice in this world!"

The council commanders looked on in astonishment. Finally the Ataman stepped in front of them.

"Zaporozhian brothers!" he said. "I would like to make a speech."

"Speak!"

"Word has it—and you may well know more about this than I do—that many Zaporozhians have run up such debts in the stores of the Jews and their cohorts that no devil will give them any more credit. Word also has it that there are many young fellows whose eyes have never seen battle, and, as we all know, a young man cannot make do without war. What kind of Zaporozhian can he be if he has never killed a heathen?"

"He speaks well," Bulba muttered to himself.

"I do not want you to think that I am speaking these words in order to break the peace! God forbid! I am only saying what I see and hear. We have a church here, but it would be sheer blasphemy to put into words what a disgraceful state it is in! By God's good grace, the Sech has been located here for many years, and yet the church is completely unadorned, its icons lacking the simplest chasubles. It has not crossed anyone's mind to create a single silver mounting for an icon. All the church has ever received is what the Cossacks have bequeathed it, not that this has ever amounted to much, for a Cossack will drink up everything during his lifetime. I am not saying this so that we should go to war with the heathens—we promised the Sultan peace, and it would be a great sin if we broke our promise, because we swore to it by our faith."

"Why is he complicating things?" Bulba muttered to himself.

"So you see, brothers, why we cannot start a war. Our chivalric honor will not allow it. My understanding is limited, but what I'm wondering is, should we send our young men off alone in our skiffs to raid the Anatolian shores? What do you think, brothers?"

"We will all go! Take us all to the Anatolian shores!" men shouted from all sides. "We will lay down our lives for the True Faith!"

The Ataman looked startled, as if the last thing he wanted was to rouse the whole Sech to arms, for it would be wrong to break the pledge of peace given to the Sultan.

"Brothers! May I make another speech?"

"Enough!" the Zaporozhians shouted. "You have already spoken the best words that can be spoken!"

"If that is how things are, then so be it! I bow to your will. As we all know, and as the Holy Writ proclaims, the voice of the people is the voice of God. One cannot contrive anything more clever than what the people have contrived. But keep one thing in mind: The Sultan will doubtless punish the pleasure our young men are to enjoy. We will have to prepare ourselves, and be at our strongest! We must fear no one! And while we are away the Tatars might well attack! Those Turk dogs don't dare look you in the eye, they don't dare come to a house when the master is home, but they will all too gladly creep up behind you and bite you in the heel, and their bite is raw indeed! As we have come this far in our decision, I must speak the truth and own that we do not have enough crushed gunpowder or skiffs for all of us to go into battle. But I am well pleased, and bow to your wishes!"

The cunning Ataman fell silent. Groups of Cossacks began talking, and company captains conferred with one another. Fortunately, not many of the men were drunk, and so it was decided to follow the Ataman's prudent words.

A few of the Cossacks set out immediately for the opposite bank of the Dnieper, to where the Sech treasury and the weapons that had been seized from the enemy lay concealed in unreachable burrows and under water. Others rushed to the skiffs to inspect them and prepare them for the expedition. The shore quickly filled with a crowd. A few carpenters appeared, carrying axes. Old, sunburned Cossacks, broad-shouldered and thick-legged, with graying or black mustaches, stood up to their knees in the water with rolled-up trousers, and dragged the skiffs into the river with sturdy ropes. Others were hauling dry logs and trees of all shapes and sizes. Skiffs were being patched up with planks and turned upside down to be caulked and tarred; bundles of reeds were tied to their sides so they would not capsize at sea. Rows of bonfires were lit some distance inland from the shore, and tar was boiling in copper cauldrons. The old and the experienced taught the young. Hammering and shouts spread all around. The teeming banks swayed and moved.

A large ferry neared the shore. On it stood a crowd of men, who had begun waving from afar. They were Cossacks in ragged tunics. Their disorderly getup—many stood smoking their pipes in nothing but their shirts—showed that they had either just escaped a calamity, or had been carousing with such abandon that they had drunk the very clothes off their backs. A squat, broad-shouldered Cossack of about fifty stepped from their midst and stood before them. He shouted and waved more vehemently than the rest, but his words were inaudible above the hammering and yelling of the workers on the shore.

"What brings you here?" the Ataman asked when the ferry reached the shore.

All the men stopped working and, putting down their axes and chisels, looked on expectantly.

"A disaster!" the squat Cossack shouted from the ferry.

"What disaster?"

"Brother Zaporozhians, may I give a speech?"

"Speak!"

"Or would you rather call together an assembly?"

"Speak! We are all here."

Everyone gathered in a crowd by the ferry.

"Can it be that you haven't heard what is happening in our lands?"

"What is happening?" one of the Sech commanders asked.

"What, he asks! Can it be that the Tatars have stuffed your ears with plaster and you have heard nothing?"

"Well, tell us what happened!"

"Things have happened the like of which we haven't seen since we were born and baptized!"

"So tell us what happened, you son of a bitch!" someone in the crowd shouted, obviously losing patience.

"As things stand, our own holy churches no longer belong to us!"

"What do you mean, they no longer belong to us?"

"The Jews are holding them in pledge. If you don't place money in the Jew's hand, there is no midday mass!"

"What are you babbling about?"

"And if a dog of a Jew does not scratch a sign with his unclean hand on our holy Easter cake, then we won't be able to bless the Easter cake either."

"He is lying, brothers! It cannot be that an unclean Jew would scratch a sign on our Easter cake!"

"Hear me, for there is something else, too! Popish priests are swarming over the whole of the Ukraine in carts! The evil is not that they are traveling in carts, but that they have harnessed Orthodox Christian men instead of horses! Hear me, for there is something else, too! They say the Jews' women have begun sewing themselves skirts from our priests' cassocks! This is how things stand in the Ukraine, brothers, while you are carousing here in Zaporozhe, for it seems the Tatar has driven such fear into you that you have neither eyes nor ears, and do not hear what is happening in the world!"

"Stop, stop!" the Ataman shouted. He had been listening with eyes fixed on the ground like all the other Zaporozhians, who in important matters never gave in to their first impulses but remained silent, their silence fueling the grim power of their fury. "Stop, and I shall speak! May the devil snatch your fathers, but what were you doing when all this happened? Where were your sabers? How could you let such lawlessness pass?"

"How could we let such lawlessness pass? You try and stand up to fifty thousand Poles! And then, sin will out, many dogs from our side went over to their faith!"

"What about your Ataman and commanders, what did they do?"

"God save us from what they did!"

"What did they do?"

"Our Ataman ended up being roasted inside a copper cauldron and now lies in Warsaw, and the hands and heads of our commanders are being paraded at fairs! That is what our commanders allowed to happen!"

The crowd stirred. First a hush, such as heralds a fierce storm, lay over the shore, and then loud words rose and the whole shore burst into speech.

"The Jews are holding our churches in pledge?"

"Popish priests have harnessed Orthodox Christians to carts?"

"How can we bear such tortures from the damn nonbelievers on Russian soil?"

"How can we allow them to do such things to an Ataman and to commanders!"

"We cannot let this pass!"

"We cannot!"

Such words came flying from all sides. The Zaporozhians felt their strength mounting. This was no longer the emotion of a wild and careless group, but that of strong, sturdy men slow to flare up, but when they did, the fire within them raged resolute and long.

"Hang the Jews!" someone in the crowd yelled. "We will not have their women make skirts out of our priests' cassocks! We will not have them mark our Easter cake. Drown the rascals in the Dnieper!"

These words darted like lightning through the crowd, and the Cossacks surged toward the settlement to slaughter the Jews.

The poor sons of Israel, losing the little courage they had, hid in empty vodka barrels and inside stoves; they even crawled beneath the skirts of their women. But the Cossacks found them all.

"Most exalted and illustrious gentlemen!" shouted one of the Jews, tall and thin as a stick, his pitiful face, twisted with fear, jutting out of a heap of people. "Illustrious gentlemen! Let us speak! Just a word or two! We will tell you things you have never yet heard, things so important, words cannot describe how important!"

"Let them speak!" Bulba said. He always liked to hear what the accused had to say.

"Illustrious gentlemen, gentlemen the like of which the world has never before seen," the Jew spluttered, "no, by God, never ever before seen! The best, the kindest and most valiant gentlemen in the whole world!" His voice faltered and trembled with fear. "How can you even think we ever disliked the Zaporozhians? The men going about the Ukraine putting everything under pledge are not our people! By God, they are not! The devil knows who they might be, but they are not Jews in any way! They should be spat at and chased away! The men here next to me agree, don't you, Shloyme, Shmul?"

"By God, he is right!" Shloyme and Shmul, white as chalk, their yarmulkes tattered, called from the crowd.

"We have never yet hobnobbed with your enemies," the lanky Jew continued. "And as for the Catholics, we want nothing to do with them, may the devil visit them in their dreams! To us all Zaporozhians are like our very own brothers—"

"What! Zaporozhians your brothers!" someone yelled from the crowd. "You won't live to see the day, you damn Jews! Into the Dnieper with them! Drown the whole lot!"

These words were like a signal. The Cossacks grabbed the Jews by the arms and hurled them into the river. Pitiful shouts came from all around, but the grim Zaporozhians only laughed at the sight of the Jews' shod and stockinged legs flailing in the air. The poor orator, realizing that he had tightened the noose of disaster around his own neck, jumped out of his caftan, by which the Cossacks had grabbed him and, in his tight, brightly colored camisole, threw himself on the ground and grasped Bulba's foot.

"Great lord and most illustrious gentleman! I knew your deceased brother, Dorosha! He was a soldier who was an ornament of chivalry! I gave him eight hundred gold ducats when he had to buy himself out of the Turk's captivity!"

"You knew my brother?" Taras asked.

"By God, I did! He was a bighearted gentleman!"

"What is your name?"

"Yankel."

"Very well," Taras said, and then, after a moment's thought, turned to the Cossacks. "There'll be time enough to hang this Jew later if we need to, but for now give him to me."

Taras took Yankel to his cart, beside which his Cossacks were standing.

"Crawl under there and don't move! And you, brothers, don't let the Jew get away."

Taras Bulba headed for the square where all the Cossacks had gathered. As they were now to set out on a land campaign, they had all left the shore and the skiffs; they no longer needed boats, but rather carts and horses. Everyone, young and old, wanted to march on the campaign. All, together with the council of commanders, the captains, the Ataman, and the will of the whole Zaporozhian army, decided to march on Poland to avenge the evil that had come upon the Ukraine and the shaming of the True Faith and Cossack glory, to loot the towns, set fire to villages and granaries, and spread Cossack glory far over the steppes. Everyone was strapping on gear and armor. The Ataman had grown a good two feet in stature. He was no longer the soft-spoken executor of the erratic will of the men who had elected him. He was now the absolute ruler, the despot. All the headstrong, carousing knights now stood neatly in rows, their heads respectfully lowered. They did not dare raise their eyes when the Ataman gave his orders, and he gave them in a quiet and unruffled tone, never raising his voice, in the measured words of an old, experienced Cossack who was, not for the first time, executing a cleverly thought-out enterprise.

"Check everything, check everything well," he said. "Check your carts and the tar for the wheels, try out your weapons. Do not take too many clothes with you, just a shirt and two trousers, and a pot of flour paste and one of ground millet. I don't want anyone to take more with him. All the provisions we need will be kept on our supply carts. I want every Cossack to have two horses. And we will take two hundred pair of oxen, for we will need them when we get to river crossings and swamps. And what is most important, I want you to keep order! I know that there are those among you who, the moment God sends some loot your way, will drop everything to shred Chinese silks and precious velvets into foot wrappings. Avoid such devilish ways, do not loot women's clothes and the like! Take only weapons that look good to you, and silver and gold coins, because they are easy to carry and will always be of use. And I will tell you one thing in advance: If anyone gets drunk during the campaign, then nothing will save him. He will be tethered to a cart like a dog, regardless of who he is, and even if he is the most valiant Cossack of our whole army, he will be shot then and there and left lying as carrion for the birds, because a drunkard on a campaign does not deserve Christian burial! I want all young men to listen always to their elders! If you are grazed by a bullet, or if a saber grazes your head or any other part of your body, then you must not pay too much attention to it. Just mix a measure of gunpowder with a cup of vodka, drink it down, and there'll be no fever and all will be well. As for your wound, if it's not too big just spit in your palm, rub some earth in it, and smear the dirt on the wound—that'll dry it out. Well, to work, to work, my boys! Don't hurry yourselves, take care of everything nice and slow!"

The Ataman finished his speech and the Cossacks immediately set to work. The whole Sech sobered up and not a single drunken man was to be found, as if there had never been a drunken Cossack. Some busied themselves fixing wheels and changing axles, others hauled sacks of provisions onto some carts, weapons onto others, and rounded up horses and oxen. From all corners echoed hooves, shots from muskets being tried out, the clanging of sabers, the lowing of oxen, the creaking of rolling carts, words and heated voices, and the goading of beasts. Soon the Cossack horde stretched far and wide over the field, and it would have been quite a feat for a man to run from its head to its tail.

In the small wooden church the priest held mass and sprinkled holy water over the men. All kissed the cross. When the army moved and marched out of the Sech, the Zaporozhians turned and looked back one last time.

"Farewell, Mother Sech!" they shouted. "May God protect you from all misfortune!"

As they rode through the settlement, Taras Bulba saw how his Jew, Yankel, had set up a makeshift booth with an awning and was selling flint, gunpowder, and all kinds of military supplies necessary for the campaign. He was even selling bread and buns.

"That devil of a Jew!" Taras muttered to himself, and rode over to him.

"You idiot! What are you doing sitting here like a target for somebody's musket? You're begging to be picked off like a sparrow from its twig!"

Yankel quickly sidled up to Taras and motioned conspiratorially with both hands. "Your Excellency, as long as you don't tell anyone. You see, I have my own cart hidden among the Cossack ones, and in it

I'm carrying all kinds of necessary supplies! Along the way I will sell provisions at prices lower than any Jew has ever managed. By God I will, yes, by God I will!"

Taras Bulba shrugged his shoulders, amazed at the feistiness of the Jewish spirit, and rode back to join the Cossack horde.

5

Soon the whole southwest of Poland fell prey to terror. Word spread like wildfire: "The Zaporozhians are coming! The Zaporozhians!" Everyone who could flee did so. People snatched up their belongings and ran, as they always did during that discordant and unreflective century in which men built neither castles nor fortresses but lived in makeshift straw-covered huts. "Why waste time and money on a house that will be destroyed in one of the next Tatar raids?" people said. Everyone was in a panic. Some exchanged their oxen and plows for a horse and musket and set out for their regiments; others chased away their livestock and hid themselves, taking with them only what they could carry. At times one met along the road those who were ready to face the invaders with musket in hand, but there were many more who had already fled. Everyone knew how difficult it was to counter the violent, warring horde known as the Zaporozhian army, which despite its seemingly erratic disorder had a structure designed for battle. The horsemen rode without wearing out the horses, the infantry marched soberly behind the carts, and the whole army moved only at night, resting during the day in wildernesses and uninhabited areas and forests, which in those days were abundant. Scouts and spies were sent out ahead to assess the lay of the land. More often than not, the Zaporozhians appeared where they were least expected, and then everyone in their path had to bid farewell to life. Fires engulfed villages. Horses and livestock that had not been herded off before the army arrived were slaughtered on the spot. It seemed that the Cossacks were on a carousing rampage rather than a campaign. Today one's hair would stand on end at the terrible violence they wrought in that brutish century. Slaughtered infants, women whose breasts were slashed off, captive men who were released with the skin peeled off from their knees down to their toes. The Cossacks, one could say, were paying back old debts with harsh coin indeed. The prelate of one of the monasteries, hearing of the Cossacks' advance, sent two of his monks to advise them that they should not behave in this way, that there was a treaty between the Zaporozhians and the government, and that they were breaking their promise to the King, and also trampling on people's rights.

"Tell the prelate from me and from all the Zaporozhians that he need not worry," the Ataman said. "We are just lighting our pipes; there is much more to come."

Soon the magnificent abbey was in flames, its colossal Gothic windows staring austerely through the rolling waves of fire. The running crowds of monks, Jews, and women flooded towns where garrisons and fortifications might still offer some hope. What belated help the government periodically sent, in the form of small regiments, either could not find the Cossacks, or on encountering them lost their nerve, turned on their heels, and galloped away on their valiant steeds.

There were also a number of the Polish King's generals who, triumphant in earlier campaigns, decided to join forces and face the Zaporozhians head-on. It was here that Taras Bulba's two sons, who shunned the plundering and marauding and the skirmishes with a powerless enemy, and who were eager to impress their elders, proved themselves. They fought hand to hand with the spirited and vain-glorious Poles, who were parading on their haughty horses, the long, folded-back sleeves of their mantles fluttering in the wind. It was good sport. Ostap and Andri acquired many bridles, precious sabers, and weapons. They had matured within a single month, completely trans-formed from fledglings whose feathers had just sprouted to full-grown men. Their features, which until now had retained some of the soft-ness of youth, became stern and strong. Taras was happy to see that his sons were among the foremost fighters. From the day he was born, Ostap had seemed made for a warrior's life and the difficult task of performing heroic feats. Not once did he lose his head, nor was he caught off guard by any situation. He could gauge danger in a flash, with a coolness almost unnatural in a twenty-two-year-old, instantly finding means to evade it, but only in order to deal with it more effec-tively. His every movement was already marked by confidence, and it was clear that he had the makings of a future leader. His body exuded strength, and his chivalric qualities already had in them a lion's prowess.

"He will make a good general one day!" old Bulba said. "By God, he will make such a good general that his own father won't reach up to his belt!"

Bulba's younger son, Andri, immersed himself in the bewitching music of bullets and swords. He knew neither forethought nor plan-ning, nor did he ever pause to gauge his own strength or that of his op-ponent. Battle for Andri was crazed bliss and drunkenness. He was transformed—his head blazed; everything before his eyes flashed and flickered as horses fell thundering to the ground; heads rolled; and he rode intoxicated through the whistle of bullets and the flashing of sabers, striking out left and right, not heeding the blows that were dealt him. More than once Taras watched in astonishment as Andri, driven by a burning passion, faced situations that a levelheaded, ratio-nal man never could, his crazed onslaught bringing about miracles that bewildered even the most battle-tried warriors.

"He is a good fighter, too! The enemy will never lay hands on him!" old Bulba said to himself in amazement. "He isn't Ostap, but he's a good, a very good fighter indeed!"

The army decided to head straight for the town of Dubno where, word had it, many rich men lived and much treasure was to be had. After a day and a half of marching the Zaporozhians arrived at the town. The townsfolk decided to defend themselves to the last man, preferring to die in the streets and squares and on their doorsteps rather than allow the enemy into their houses. A high earthen rampart surrounded the town. Where the rampart was lower, stone walls or houses or simply an oak palisade rose, serving as a battery. The garrison stationed in Dubno was strong, and aware of the importance of their mission.

The Zaporozhians wanted to charge the ramparts, but were driven back by powerful grapeshot. The townsfolk, great and small, had no intention of standing idly by, and crowded onto the ramparts. A desperate resistance flashed in their eyes. The womenfolk were also resolved to help, raining stones, pots, barrels, and boiling pitch onto the Zaporozhians' heads, and even sacks of sand that blinded them. The Zaporozhians did not like storming fortifications, and abhorred laying siege.

"Very well, brothers, let us retreat!" the Ataman said to his fellow Cossacks. "But may I be a rascal of a Tatar and not a Christian at all if we let a single man leave this town! Let those dogs die of hunger!"

The army retreated, surrounded the whole town and, having nothing better to do, began devastating the surrounding area, torching villages and fields of grain. They released herds of horses onto fields still untouched by the sickle where, as if on purpose, thick sheaves of grain swayed, an uncommonly good crop. The town watched in horror as the foundation of its existence was destroyed.

The Zaporozhians had lined up their carts in two rows around the town. They formed themselves into companies, just as they did at the Sech, smoked their pipes, exchanged looted weapons, played leapfrog and odds-and-evens, and gazed at the town with lethal coolness. At night they lit campfires. Cooks in every company boiled kasha in large copper cauldrons. A watch stood next to the fires that burned throughout the night. But soon the Zaporozhians began to grow restless from all the inactivity and the prolonged sobriety without fighting. The Ataman even ordered the doubling of vodka rations, which were dispensed to the army whenever there were no difficult assaults or imminent marches. The young men, and especially Taras Bulba's sons, did not like this kind of life. Andri was visibly bored.

"You foolish boy," Taras said to him. "A Cossack who can wait in calm patience will in time become Ataman! A good warrior is not just a man who doesn't lose his head at a crucial moment; a good warrior is a man who doesn't fall into boredom when there is nothing to do, but endures everything! Try as you might to sway such a man, he will stand his ground!"

But fiery youth will not see eye-to-eye with an old man. The two have different natures and will look at the same thing differently.

In the meantime Taras's regiment arrived, led by Tovkach, who was accompanied by two captains, a scribe, and other regimental ranks. He had assembled more than four thousand Cossacks. There were also quite a few volunteers among them, who had joined of their own free will the moment they heard what was at stake, without even being conscripted. The captains brought Taras's sons the blessing of their aged mother, and for each of them a small icon of cypress wood from the Mezhigorsk Monastery in Kiev. The two brothers, preoccupied in spite of themselves as they thought of their mother, hung the holy icons around their necks. Did her blessing signify something? Did her blessing bode victory over the enemy and a cheerful return to their native soil with bounty and glory that would be celebrated in the eternal epics of the bandura bards? Or did their mother's blessing foretell something else? But the future is unknown and lies before man like an autumn fog rising from the swamps, a fog in which birds fly high and low, fluttering their wings and not recognizing one another, the dove not seeing the hawk, the hawk not seeing the dove, neither knowing how near or far it might be from its destruction.

Ostap had returned to his company. But Andri, without knowing why, felt a heaviness in his heart. The Cossacks had finished their dinner, and evening had long since faded. A beautiful July night embraced the air, but Andri did not return to his company. He could not lie down to sleep, but was compelled to gaze at the picture before him. Countless stars flickered in the sky with their sharp delicate shimmer. Carts bearing grimy tar buckets and heaped with all the goods and provisions seized from the enemy were strewn over the field. Everywhere, next to the carts, under them, near them, Zaporozhians were stretched out on the grass. They were all sleeping in striking positions, their heads resting on sacks, on lambskin hats, or on a comrade's hip. A saber, a pistol, a short-tipped pipe with brass trim, and a flint lay beside every Cossack. Heavy oxen, their legs tucked under them, lay in large whitish clumps and from a distance looked like gray stones scattered over the rises and dips of the fields. The thick snoring of the sleeping army rose from the grass and was echoed by the light neighing of stallions in the fields, indignant over their tethered legs. And yet a majestic but threatening element seeped into the beauty of this July night. It was the glow of the settlements burning in the distance. In one area the flames spread calmly and regally over the sky. In another, they engulfed something flammable and suddenly tore and whistled like a whirlwind soaring upward to the stars, shredded tufts expiring in the farthest reaches of the sky.

There before Andri stood the black, gutted monastery, grim as a Cartesian monk, showing its sinister grandeur with every reflection. There before him the monastery orchards were burning. He thought he heard the trees, cloaked in smoke, hissing, and when the flames flared up they suddenly cast a fiery, lilac, phosphorescent light over clusters of ripe plums. Here and there they turned yellowing pears into pure gold. Among them, the bodies of poor Jews and monks who had perished in the fire hung black from the burnt-out building's walls and wooden beams. Birds circled high over the flames, like a swarm of dark and delicate crosses above the blazing field.

The besieged town seemed asleep. Its steeples, roofs, paling, and walls flickered quietly in the light of the distant blaze. Andri walked through the rows of Cossacks. The campfires where the watchmen sat were dying down, and the watchmen were dozing, having sated their Cossack appetites with kasha and dumplings. Andri was taken aback by so much nonchalance. "We are lucky there is no powerful enemy nearby and that we have nobody to fear!" he thought.

Finally he walked over to one of the carts, climbed onto it, and lay down on his back with his hands behind his head. But he could not fall asleep, and gazed for a long time at the sky that lay spread out before him. The air was fresh and clear. The Milky Way's thicket of stars, bursting with light, stretched like a sash across the sky. At times Andri seemed to doze, and for an instant the faint mist of slumber veiled the sky, but then the veil fell away again and he could see the sky clearly.

Suddenly he sensed a human countenance shimmering strangely before him. He thought it was an apparition of sleep, and that it would disappear. He opened his eyes wider and saw an emaciated face leaning down toward him, looking him straight in the eye. Long hair, black as coal, fell in an unkempt tangle from a dark, hastily tied kerchief. The strange glint of the eyes and the deathly pallor of the face with its stark features seemed to be those of a ghost. He instinctively reached for his musket.

"Who are you?" he gasped convulsively. "What unclean spirit might you be? Away with you! If you are a living man, then you have chosen a bad time for joking! I'll finish you off with a single shot!"

The apparition raised a finger to its lips, as if begging him to be silent. Andri let go of his weapon and peered at the apparition more carefully. From the long hair, the neck, and the dark, half-exposed breast he saw that it was a woman. But she could not be from these lands. Her face was weathered, and worn with privation. Her high cheekbones stood out above her sunken cheeks, and her narrow eyes slanted upward in a sharp arch. The longer he peered at her features the more he felt there was something familiar about them.

"Who are you? It seems to me I know you or have seen you somewhere," he finally asked.

"Two years ago in Kiev."

"Two years ago … in Kiev …" Andri repeated, trying to recall what little remained in his memory of his life as a student. He looked at her again closely.

"You are the Tatar! The Tatar maid of the young lady, the governor's daughter!" he suddenly shouted.

"Hush!" the Tatar woman gasped, clasping her hands together with an imploring look in her eyes. Her whole body shook, and she quickly looked behind her to see if anyone had been awakened.

"Tell me … tell me why you are here!" Andri whispered breathlessly, his words faltering with emotion. "Where is the young lady? Is she still alive?"

"She is here in the town."

"In the town?" he gasped, barely managing to check his voice, feeling the blood gushing into his heart. "Why is she here in this town?"

"Because her father is here. He has been the governor of Dubno for a year and a half now."

"Is she married? Tell me! Is she married, yes or no?"

"For two days now she hasn't had a bite to eat."

"What do you mean?"

"For a long time the townsfolk haven't had as much as a crust of bread, and are now eating earth."

Andri was struck dumb.

"The young lady saw you among the Zaporozhians from the town's ramparts. She said to me: 'Tell him to come if he remembers me— and if he does not remember me, then tell him to give you a piece of bread for my poor old mother, because I do not want to see her die before my eyes. I would rather be the first one to die. Beg him, kneel before him. He, too, has an aged mother—let him give you a piece of bread for her sake!' "

Feelings of every kind flared up in the Cossack's heart.

"But how did you get here?"

"Through an underground passage."

"There's an underground passage?"

"There is."

"Where?"

"You will not betray me, will you, young knight?"

"I swear by the Holy Cross that I will not!"

"If you go down into the ravine and cross the stream, you'll find it among the reeds."

"And it leads all the way into the town?"

"Yes, it leads right into the town monastery."

"Let's go, let's go immediately!"

"But for the love of Christ and of Holy Mary, give me a piece of bread!"

"I will. Stay here, next to the cart. Or, better, get into the cart and lie down so that nobody will see you—anyway, everyone's asleep. I'll come back right away."

He went to the carts in which the company provisions were kept. His heart was pounding. Everything of the past, everything that had been smothered by the hard life of war, the current Cossack bivouacs—it all came floating to the surface, drowning everything of the present. Once more the image of the proud young woman emerged before him as if from the dark depths of the ocean. Again her beautiful arms shimmered in his memory, her eyes, her laughing mouth, her thick, chestnut-colored hair tumbling in curls over her breasts, her lithe, harmonious limbs. No, they had not faded, they had not disappeared from his heart; they had only moved to the side for a while in order to make way for other powerful emotions. But often the young Cossack's deepest sleep had been troubled by these images.

And often, waking with a start, he lay sleepless on his straw unable to understand what was happening to him.

He walked to the carts. His knees shook, and his heart pounded faster at the thought that he would see her again. He came to the carts unable to remember why he had come. He raised his hand and rubbed his forehead, trying to recall what it was he had to do. He shuddered, filled with fear. His mind cleared. She was starving to death! He seized a few large black loaves of bread from one of the carts, but suddenly wondered whether such bread, though good enough for a robust Zaporozhian, would not be too rough for a constitution as delicate as hers. He suddenly remembered that only a day ago the Ataman had reproached the cooks for having boiled all the buckwheat at once into kasha, when it could have lasted for three meals. Certain that he would find enough kasha in the cauldrons, he went to fetch his father's field kettle and took it to the cook of his company, who was sleeping by two large cauldrons, beneath which the ash was still warm. He looked into them, and to his horror saw that they were empty. It was an inhuman feat for a company, particularly one with fewer men than most others, to have managed to devour all that food. He looked into the cauldrons of the other companies, but they were all empty, too. He remembered the saying: "Zaporozhians are like children—when there are a few crumbs of food they will gobble them up, and when there are mountains of food, again nothing will be left." What was he to do? He remembered that somewhere, perhaps in his father's cart, there were some sacks of white bread that they had found while ransacking the monastery bakery. He hurried to his father's cart, but the sacks were no longer there. Ostap lay stretched out next to the cart and was using them as a pillow, his snores echoing over the field. Andri took hold of the sacks with one hand and yanked them away. Ostap's head knocked against the ground, and he sat up half asleep, his eyes still closed.

"Stop him! Stop that damn Pole! Catch his horse! His horse!" he shouted with all his might.

"Shut up or I'll kill you!" Andri yelled in fright, raising the sack ready to strike him. But Ostap fell silent again and began to snore with such force that his breath sent shivers through the weeds among which he lay. Andri looked timidly about in case Ostap's shouts had awakened someone. The forelocked head of a Cossack from a neighboring company peered around sleepily for a moment, but then disappeared again in the weeds. Andri waited a few minutes, and finally returned laden with sacks. The Tatar woman was lying on his cart, barely breathing.

"Get up, we're going! Don't be afraid, everyone's fast asleep," he said. "Will you carry one or two of the loaves if I can't manage them all?" He heaved the sacks onto his shoulder and, pulling another one off a cart as he passed, also gathered up the loaves he had asked the Tatar woman to carry. Bent under the weight, he walked dauntlessly through the rows of sleeping Cossacks.

"Andri!" old Bulba called out as Andri walked past him. Andri's heart froze, and he stopped dead in his tracks.

"Yes?" he said quietly, his whole body shaking.

"You've got a woman with you! Wait till I get up, you'll get the hiding of your life! Women are nothing but trouble!" Taras Bulba leaned his head on his hand and stared at the Tatar woman bundled up in her shawl. Andri stood before his father more dead than alive, unable to look him in the eye, but when he finally looked up, he saw that old Bulba was fast asleep, his head still propped on his hand.

He crossed himself. Fear drained out of his heart even faster than it had flooded in. When he turned around to look at the Tatar woman, he saw that she was standing wrapped up in her shawl like a statue of dark granite, and the reflections of the distant, flaring fires lit only her eyes, stony as those of a corpse. He tugged at her sleeve and they walked on, constantly glancing behind themselves, until they finally reached the slope that led into the gully, almost a ravine, at the base of which a stream overgrown with tussocks of sedge crept lazily.

When they descended into the gully, they could no longer be seen from the field where the Zaporozhian army had set up camp. Turning to look, Andri saw that the slope behind him rose in a steep wall higher than a man. A few tufts of field grass swayed on its edge, and above them the moon rose, a tilted sickle of pure shining gold. A light breeze from the steppe heralded the approach of dawn. Yet nowhere was a cock's crow to be heard: not a single cockerel had remained either in the town or in the ravaged settlements around it.

They crossed the stream on a narrow plank and reached the opposite bank, which rose in a sheer precipice, higher than the bank behind them. This seemed the strongest and most secure point of the town's fortifications, even though the earthen rampart was lower here, and there was no sign of the garrison on it. Some distance away rose the thick monastery walls. The steep bank was overgrown with weeds; in a small hollow that lay between the precipice and the river, reeds grew almost as tall as a man. On top of the precipice stood the remains of a wicker fence that had once surrounded a vegetable garden. In front of the fence grew broad-leaved burdocks, and behind it grew goosefoot, wild prickly thistles, and sunflowers that poked their heads up higher than the rest. Here the Tatar woman took off her slippers and walked barefoot, carefully lifting the hem of her dress because the ground was swampy and covered in water. They made their way through the reeds and stopped in front of a heap of twigs and brushwood, behind which was a sort of burrow with an opening not much larger than that of a bread oven. The Tatar woman bent down and entered first. Andri followed her, crouching as low as he could to crawl through with all his sacks. Soon they were in complete darkness.

6

Andri stumbled through the dark and narrow dirt corridor behind the Tatar woman, the sacks of bread slung over his shoulder.

"Soon we'll be able to see again," she said. "We've almost come to the place where I left my lantern."

The dark earthen walls gradually grew lighter. They reached a small area that seemed to be some kind of chapel—at least, a narrow table that looked like an altar was fastened to the wall, with an almost completely faded painting of a Catholic Madonna hanging above it, lit by the flickering beams of a small silver lamp. The Tatar woman bent forward and picked up a copper lantern with a long narrow base, around which hung little chains with scissors, a needle for tending the flame, and a snuffer. She lit the lantern with the flame of the silver lamp. The light grew stronger and they walked on, at times brightly lit, at times plunged into coal-black shadows, the scene reminiscent of a painting by Gherardo Della Notte.* Andri's handsome face, blossom-

* The byname of the Dutch painter Gerrit van Honthorst (1590–1656).

ing with freshness and youth, contrasted starkly with his companion's pale, worn-out countenance. The passage grew a little wider, and Andri found he no longer had to crouch. He stared at the earthen walls, remembering the Kiev catacombs. Here, too, there were hollows in the walls, some of them containing coffins. Human bones were strewn about, sodden with dampness and decay. Saintly people had hidden here from the storms, sorrows, and seductions of life. Some places were so damp that there was water beneath the feet of Andri and the Tatar woman. He had to stop many times to let her rest, as she was repeatedly overcome by weariness. She was no longer used to food, and the small piece of bread she had devoured made her stomach ache. She kept stopping and standing still for a few moments. Finally they came to a small iron door.

"Thank God we have arrived," the Tatar woman said weakly.

She raised her hand to knock, but did not have the strength. Andri rapped loudly on the door and, hearing the sound resonate, imagined that there must be a large hall behind the door, the echo changing as it resounded off the high vaults. A few minutes later there was a clanking of keys and the sound of someone descending stairs. The door opened, and they saw a monk with keys and a candle standing on a narrow staircase. Andri involuntarily stepped back at the sight of a Catholic monk, a sight that always awoke such hatred and contempt in Cossacks that they dealt with them even more brutally than they did with Jews. The monk, seeing a Cossack, also staggered back, but a quick whispered word from the Tatar woman calmed him. He locked the door, made light for them, and led them up the staircase, and they found themselves beneath the high vaults of the monastery cathedral. A priest was kneeling and praying quietly in front of an altar on which stood tall candelabras with burning candles. On either side of the priest two choirboys with frilled shirts and purple robes knelt, holding censers. The priest was praying for a miracle from heaven: that God would save the town, would strengthen the people's sinking spirits, would send them forbearance, would chase away the evil tempter who made men fainthearted and grumble and shed tears over worldly misfortune. A few ghostlike women knelt in the pews, propping themselves up on chair backs and dark wooden benches. A few men were also kneeling sorrowfully, slumped against the columns and pillars that supported the side vaults. The rosy flush of dawn suddenly lit the stained-glass window above the altar, and many-colored curls of light fell on the floor, illuminating the dark church. The whole altar in its deep niche was suddenly bathed in light. Incense hung in the air, a cloud of rainbow brightness. From his dark corner Andri gazed in amazement at this miracle of light. Suddenly the majestic roar of the organ filled the church, growing deeper and deeper, swelling, changing into a powerful peal of thunder and then suddenly becoming heavenly music that soared up to the cathedral's vaults, its chanting tones like the high voices of girls—and, turning again into powerful thunder, it fell silent. For a long time the sound rose trembling to the vaults, and Andri stood dumbstruck with amazement at the majesty of the music. He felt a tug at the sleeve of his caftan.

"We have to go!" the Tatar woman said.

They walked unnoticed through the church and went out onto the square. The flush of dawn had already lit the sky, heralding the rising sun. The square was completely empty. There were still wooden stalls strewn over it, indicating that there might have been a food market here as late as a week ago. The streets, which in those days were not cobbled, were covered in dried mud. The square was surrounded by small single-story houses of stone or clay, their wooden stakes, posts, and beams visible over the walls as was the fashion in those days, and which can still be seen today in some Lithuanian and Polish towns. The houses had disproportionately high roofs with many oriels and dormer windows. On one side of the square, almost next to the church, stood a building that was taller and quite distinct, most probably the town hall or some other place of government. It was two stories high, and had a gallery with two arched windows and a clock whose face was cut into the roof. The square lay desolate, but Andri, to his surprise, heard quiet moans. He looked about and saw two or three people lying almost motionless on the ground on the far side of the square. He went closer to see if they were asleep or dead, and his foot suddenly knocked against something. It was the dead body of a woman, apparently a Jewess. She seemed to have been young, even though it was not clear from her distorted, emaciated features. Over her hair she wore a red silk kerchief, its seam adorned by two rows of little pearls or beads. A few long and curly locks hung down over her thin neck with its bloated veins. Next to her lay an infant, its hand convulsively grasping for her wasted breasts, kneading them with its fingers in helpless rage at not finding milk. The infant was no longer crying or shouting, and it was only obvious from its quietly rising and falling stomach that it was still alive, though perhaps about to breathe its last.

Andri and the Tatar woman turned into one of the streets and suddenly came across a crazed man, who upon seeing Andri's precious sacks flew at him like a tiger and clung to him, shouting: "Bread!" But his strength did not match his crazed state. Andri pushed him away, and he fell. Andri took pity on him and threw him a loaf of bread. The crazed man hurled himself onto it like a rabid dog, gnawing and biting at it, and suddenly fell into terrible convulsions and died right there in the street from his long lack of food.

At almost every step they came upon terrible victims of starvation. It was as if people, no longer able to suffer the pangs of hunger within their houses, had run out into the streets, as if some kind of strength might descend upon them in the open. An old woman was sitting at the gate of one of the houses; it was impossible to tell whether she was asleep, or dead, or simply daydreaming. One thing was certain: she no longer saw or heard anything and sat motionless, her head resting on her chest. An elongated, emaciated body was hanging from the roof of another house. The poor man had been unable to bear the pangs of hunger and had preferred to hasten his death by suicide.

"Is it possible these people couldn't find anything to keep themselves alive?" Andri asked the Tatar woman when he saw these terrible testimonies of hunger. "When someone is driven to extremes he has to feed himself, even if it means eating things he would never have touched before—he can eat creatures that the law otherwise forbids him to eat; everything can be eaten."

"Everything has been eaten," she replied. "Every single animal. There are no more horses or dogs, you won't even find a mouse in the whole town. We never stored any provisions, we always brought everything in from the nearby villages."

"But can it be that people are still trying to defend the town, when they are dying such terrible deaths?"

"The governor was ready to surrender, but yesterday morning a colonel who is now in Budzhaki sent a carrier pigeon with a note telling us not to give up the town. He is coming to our rescue and is only waiting for a second colonel to arrive so they can march with joint forces. We expect them any moment now. . . . Ah, here is the house."

Andri had already seen the house from some distance, as it stood out from the rest. It looked as if it had been built by an Italian architect. It was two stories high and made of elegant brick. The windows of the first floor were framed by protruding granite encasements. The upper floor consisted entirely of small arches that formed a gallery. Coats-of-arms hung on the lattice behind the arches and also on the corners of the house. Wide steps of painted brick led from the house down to the town square, and two sentries, looking more like sculptures than living beings, sat at the base of the steps, each man with one hand leaning in picturesque symmetry on the halberd standing next to him, the other propping up his drooping head. They were not asleep or even dozing, and yet they seemed unconscious to the world. They did not even look up to see who was climbing the steps. At the top, Andri and the Tatar woman came across a heavily armed soldier with a prayer book in his hand. He raised his drained eyes, but the Tatar woman spoke a few quick words and he lowered them again to his prayer book.

They entered the front room, which was quite large and served as a reception chamber. Sitting slumped along the wall were soldiers, servants, huntsmen, cupbearers, and other courtiers, who form every Polish grandee's pompous retinue. The fumes of an expired candle hung in the air. In the middle of the room two other candles were still burning in enormous candelabras almost as tall as a man, even though morning was already peering in through the broad window.

Andri went toward an ornately carved oak door on which a coat-of-arms hung, but the Tatar woman caught hold of his sleeve and pointed to a smaller door in a side wall. They went through it into a corridor which led to a room. The light that came through a crack in the shutters fell on the crimson curtain, the gilded cornice, and the painting that hung on the wall. The Tatar woman motioned Andri to wait, and opened the door to an adjacent room from which the light of a fire shone. He heard a whisper, followed by a hushed voice that sent shivers through his whole body. He looked through the half-open door and caught a glimpse of a slender female figure, her long splendid hair falling onto her raised arm. The Tatar woman came back and told Andri to go in.

He entered the room in confusion, and the door fell shut behind him. Two candles were burning. A lamp flickered before a holy image beneath which stood a tall prayer stool in the Catholic manner, with a ledge for kneeling. But that was not what his eyes were seeking. He turned, and saw a woman who seemed to have been frozen in a quick movement, as if her whole figure had intended to fly toward him but had suddenly stopped. He stood dumbfounded before her. He had not imagined she would look like this. She was not the girl he had once known. This woman did not bear the least resemblance to her: this woman was twice as beautiful. There had been something unfinished about the girl, something incomplete, but now she had become a masterpiece that had received its final brushstroke. She had been a frivolous, pretty girl, but was now a woman at the height of her beauty. Pure feeling expressed itself in her raised eyes—not fragments or hints of feeling, but feeling at its fullest. The tears in her eyes had not yet dried, gilding them with a sparkle that touched his heart. Her breasts, neck, and shoulders had reached the wonderful precincts of a maturing beauty. Her hair, which in the past had fallen about her face in delicate curls, was now thick and rich, partly pinned up, partly falling over the whole length of her arm, tumbling in long, beautifully curled locks onto her breast. Every feature in her face had changed. Andri strove to find at least one of the traits he had kept etched in his mind, but to no avail. She was extremely pale, but this did not cast the least shadow over her beauty. On the contrary, it seemed that it gave her something irresistibly triumphant. Andri stood motionless before her, feeling in his heart a reverential dread. She, for her part, seemed struck by the sight of him in all the handsomeness and strength of his young manhood, the very motionlessness of his limbs manifesting an unbounded freedom of movement. Fiery strength flashed in his eyes, his dark eyebrows arched boldly, his youthful mustache gleamed, and his bronzed cheeks shone with the brightness of chaste fire.

"There are no words to express my gratitude, generous knight," she said, her silvery voice trembling. "Only God can thank you. I am but a weak woman. . . ." She lowered her eyes, and her eyelids, beautiful snowy arcs crested by long lashes sharp as arrows, sank with them. She lowered her exquisite face, and a delicate blush rose to her cheeks. Andri could not say a word. He wanted to express everything he felt, the passion surging within his heart. But he could not. His lips were barred and his words bereft of sound. He had been raised in the Seminary and in rough military life and, incapable of responding to her words, felt indignant at his Cossack nature.

The Tatar woman entered the room. She had cut the bread Andri had brought and put it on a gold platter, which she placed before her mistress. The beautiful woman looked at her, looked at the bread, and then raised her eyes to Andri, and there was much in those eyes. Her look, which bespoke an inability to express the feelings that overwhelmed her, was more tangible to Andri than any words could have been. His heart suddenly felt light. It was as if everything began opening out within him. Feelings stirred which until then had been under a heavy yoke but now felt liberated, free, and ready to pour out in a fierce stream of words.

Suddenly the beautiful woman turned away. "What about Mother? Did you bring her some bread?" she asked the Tatar woman with a worried air.

"She is asleep."

"And Father?"

"I brought him some bread. He said he would come to thank the knight in person."

With indescribable delight Andri watched the young woman break off a piece with her radiant fingers and raise it to her lips. He suddenly remembered the hunger-crazed man who had died before his eyes after devouring the loaf of bread he had thrown him. He turned ashen and grabbed her hand. "Don't eat any more! It has been such a long time since you have eaten that this bread will be poison to you!"

She lowered her hand and put the bread back on the platter, looking into his eyes like an obedient child. If words could only describe what is in a young woman's glance! But neither chisel, nor brush, nor the mightiest of words can capture what at times will fill a woman's look, or the tender feelings that such a glance can unleash in its recipient.

"My Czarina!" Andri exclaimed, his soul overflowing. "Say but a word and I shall do whatever your heart desires! Set me the most impossible task, the hardest task in the world, and I shall fulfill it! Tell me to do what no other man can do and I shall do it, even if I perish! I swear upon the Holy Cross that I would gladly die for you! My words fall short! I have three farms, half my father's herd, all my mother's dowry—including what she has hidden from my father—it all belongs to me! No Cossack has weapons like mine; the hilt of one of my swords alone is worth the best herd of horses and three thousand sheep. I will turn my back on all this, throw it away, give it up, burn it at a single word from you! I know I am uttering foolish words! I was raised in the Seminary and among Cossacks, and I am not used to speaking the way people speak where there are kings, princes, and grand knights. God created you above us lesser mortals, and even the noblest boyar women and their daughters stand far beneath you. We do not deserve to be your slaves, only heavenly angels can serve you!"

With growing amazement she listened to Andri's heartfelt speech, which, like a mirror, reflected the young force within his soul. Every word was powerful and rose frankly from the bottom of his heart. She leaned her beautiful face toward him and threw her wayward hair back, gazing at him with open lips. She wanted to say something but suddenly stopped, remembering who he was, his father, his brothers, his native soil—severe avengers—remembering how terrible the besieging Cossacks were and what a cruel fate awaited the whole town. Her eyes suddenly filled with tears. She picked up an embroidered silk handkerchief and covered her face with it, the cloth filling with her tears. She sat for a long time, her beautiful head leaning back, her teeth, white as snow, biting her nether lip as if she had felt the sting of a poisonous reptile's fangs. So that he would not see her despair, she did not lower the handkerchief from her face.

"Say but a single word!" Andri said, taking her soft hand in his. A sudden flame ran through his limbs at her touch, and he pressed her hand as it lay lifelessly in his. But she remained silent and did not move or lower the handkerchief from her face.

"Why are you so filled with grief? Why?"

She tore the handkerchief from her face and pulled her long hair out of her eyes. Plaintive words poured from her, her voice hushed as a breeze that rises on a warm evening and sweeps through reeds by the water in tones that rustle, delicate and dejected, a wayfarer stopping and listening with sudden sadness, unconscious of the dying evening, to the lively song of the village folk returning from the fields, and the distant rattling of a passing cart.

"Am I not to be pitied, as is my poor mother who gave birth to me? Is not the lot that has befallen me bitter indeed? O cruel Fate, my ruthless executioner! You brought to my feet the greatest noblemen, the richest lords and dukes, the most chivalrous knights of our lands, all professing their love! They would have seen it as the greatest of blessings had I bestowed my love upon them! I could have raised my hand, and the handsomest and most magnificent of face and pedigree would have been my husband. But cruel Fate did not draw my heart to any of them—it tore my heart away from the noblest heroes of our land and gave it to a foreign warrior, to our sworn enemy! O holy Mother of God, for what sins, for what terrible crimes do you persecute me so relentlessly? I was raised in abundance and rich bounty, I was nourished on the most exquisite dishes and the sweetest wines. To what avail? So that I should die a death more cruel than befalls the lowliest among men? Not only am I sentenced to such a terrible destiny, but I must also watch my own mother and father die in agony, even though I am prepared to lay down my life over and over to save them. And the worst is that before my bitter end I have to hear such sweet words and feel a love I have never felt before, words that tear my heart to pieces so that my bitter destiny now seems all the more bitter, so that life becomes all the more dear to me and death more terrible, and so that dying I would reproach both cruel Fate and the Holy Virgin!"

She fell silent, and deep despair was reflected in her face. Tormenting sadness lay in every trait, all her features, her grief-stricken brow, her downcast eyes, and the tears drying on her glowing cheeks—everything bespoke her utter despair.

"This cannot be!" Andri gasped. "It is impossible that such a bitter destiny should await the best and most beautiful of women! You were born to have men kneel before you as before a saint! No, you will not die, you cannot die! I swear by my life and everything dear to me in this world that you will not die! And if Fate cannot be foiled by force or prayer or courage, then we must die together! And I shall die first, I shall die at your heavenly feet! Only as a dead man will they tear me from you!"

She softly shook her beautiful head. "Do not deceive yourself," she said. "To my great sorrow, I know all too well that you must not love me. I know where your allegiance must lie. Your father, your comrades, your native soil are beckoning you! I and my people are your enemy!"

"I care nothing for my father, my comrades, or my native soil!" Andri shouted, rising to his full height, his voice and gestures those of an indomitable Cossack expressing his resolution. "I bear allegiance to no one, to no one at all! Who can claim that the Ukraine is my native soil? Who bequeathed it to me? A man's native soil is what his heart seeks and what is most dear to it! *You* are my native soil! I carry you in my heart and will as long as I live, and there is no Cossack in this world strong enough to rip this native soil out of me! I would sell, give away, destroy everything I have for this native soil!"

She stood still, a beautiful statue, and gazed at him, then suddenly burst into sobs, and with the exquisite feminine fervor that only a noblewoman who stirs the soul can manifest, she threw herself on his neck and wept, embracing him with her beautiful white arms.

Suddenly muffled shouts came from the street, followed by drumrolls and a blare of trumpets. Andri was oblivious to the noise. All he felt was her beautiful lips caressing him with the perfumed warmth of their breath, her tears trickling onto his cheeks, and her fragrant hair enveloping him in its dark and sparkling silk. But the Tatar woman came hurrying into the room. "We are saved, we are saved!" she shouted, crazed with joy. "Our troops are here! They have brought bread, wheat, and flour, and also Cossack prisoners!"

The two lovers did not understand what troops had arrived or what Cossack prisoners they had brought with them. Filled with celestial feelings, Andri kissed the fragrant lips close to his cheek, the fragrant lips returned his kiss, and in this blending of kisses the lovers felt what can be felt only once in a lifetime.

And so Andri was ruined, lost forever to the Cossack knighthood. Never again was he to see Zaporozhe, his father's house, or a true church of God! The Ukraine had lost the most valiant of the sons who had set out to defend her. Old Taras was to tear out tufts of his gray hair and curse the day he sired such a son.

7

Noise and commotion filled the Zaporozhian camp. At first nobody could explain how it had come to pass that enemy troops had managed to enter the town. Then it turned out that all the Cossacks of the Pereyaslav Company stationed by one of the town's side gates had been roaring drunk, and before anyone realized what was happening half the company had been cut down and the other half thrown into irons. Before any of the other companies, awakened by the noise, had time to reach for their weapons, the enemy troops were already marching through the gates, their rear lines shooting themselves free of the rabble of befuddled and half-drunk Cossacks who came lunging at them.

The Ataman called an assembly, and when all the men stood in a circle and fell silent, he removed his hat and began to speak. "You are aware, Brother Cossacks, what took place last night, and you are aware what drink has led us to, and how our enemy has defiled us! No sooner are double rations of vodka granted, you all drink yourself so senseless that the enemy of our Christian army not only makes off with your trousers, but spits in your face without your even noticing! A fine Cossack custom indeed!"

The Cossacks lowered their heads in shame. Only Kukubenko, the captain of the Nezamaikov Company, spoke up.

"One moment, Ataman!" he said. "I know it is not lawful that one should utter an objection when the Ataman speaks before the army, but if things did not happen the way they are presented, one must speak out! Your reproach to our Christian army is not quite correct. The Cossacks would be guilty and deserving of death had they become drunk during a march, during battle, or during a difficult task. But we have been waiting outside the town without anything to do, and right now we are not in a time of fasting or other period of Christian abstinence. On cannot expect men not to get drunk when there is nothing to do! Under these conditions it is not a sin! What we should do is show the enemy what it means to attack innocent men the way they did! We have already given them a good beating in the past—now we should give them such a thrashing that they won't be able to crawl home on all fours!"

The Cossacks liked Kukubenko's speech. They raised their heads, which had sunk ever lower, and many of the Cossacks began to nod and mumble their approval.

"Well, what do you say, Ataman?" Taras Bulba, who was standing near him, called out. "It seems to me that Kukubenko is right. What do you say?"

"What do I say? I say that lucky is the father who sired a son like Kukubenko! It is not great wisdom to speak reproachful words. Yet it is great wisdom to speak words that do not scorn a man down on his luck, but give him spirit, the way spurs give spirit to a horse that has drunk its fill of water. I was intending to say some rousing words myself, but Kukubenko spoke them before I did."

"These are good words!" resounded from the lines of Zaporozhians. "Good words!" Even the eldest among the Cossacks, standing in a somber row like gray doves, nodded their heads, their grizzled mustaches bobbing. "Good words indeed," they mumbled.

"It is not the Cossack way to storm these damn fortresses and clamber up or burrow under walls!" the Ataman continued. "That's something the Germans are good at! But from what we can tell, the enemy did not enter the town with a lot of supplies. They had only a few carts. The townsfolk are starving and will devour everything in no time at all. And we mustn't forget that their horses need hay, too! Perhaps one of their saints will rain down supplies from heaven, but as for their priests, all they do is pontificate! One thing is for sure, though: They'll be coming out sooner or later, so I want you to split into three groups and cover the roads coming from the three town gates. I want five companies in front of the main gate and three companies in front of the other gates. Colonel Bulba and his regiment will position themselves for an ambush, as will the Dyadkiv and Korsun Companies! I want the Titarev and Timoshev Companies to stand in reserve to the right of our transport carts, and the Sherbinov and the Steblikiv Companies to the left. And the men with the loudest and foulest mouths: I want you to leave the ranks and move forward to the walls to taunt the enemy! Those Poles are empty-headed and can't bear being jeered at! With any luck we might get them to come out right away! All captains are to check their companies. Whoever needs extra men can get them from what's left of the Pereyaslavs. Check over everything! Every Cossack is to get a single cup of vodka and a loaf of bread! Though I am sure everyone ate their fill yesterday. You all devoured so much food it's a miracle nobody's guts exploded! And a final point: If I find a tavern keeper or Jew selling a Cossack a single dram of vodka, I will hammer a pig's ear to the miscreant's forehead and hang him upside down by his feet! To work, brothers! To work!"

The men bowed deeply to the Ataman. They headed for their camps and carts and did not put their hats back on until they had walked a respectful distance. They all began to arm themselves, tried out their sabers and broadswords, poured gunpowder into their horns, pulled their carts into position, and selected horses.

Taras Bulba walked over to his regiment, wondering where Andri might be. Had he been shackled and taken captive along with the others? That couldn't be. Andri was not the kind of man to be taken alive. And yet he was not lying among the slaughtered Cossacks. Bulba walked the length of his regiment, deep in thought, and did not hear for quite a while that someone was calling him.

"Yes?" he finally said, emerging from his thoughts, and saw Yankel the Jew step in front of him.

"Your Excellency, Colonel Bulba! Your Excellency!" Yankel was saying in a hurried, faltering voice, with the air of a man with an important piece of news. "I managed to get inside the town, Colonel Bulba!"

Taras stared at the Jew in disbelief. "How the devil did you manage to get in there?"

"I'll tell you, I'll tell you," Yankel panted. "The moment I heard all the noise at dawn, what with the Cossacks shooting, I grabbed my caftan and didn't even put it on, but just hurried to where all the noise was, slipping my hands into the sleeves as I ran. You see, I wanted to find out right away what was going on and why the Cossacks were shooting so early in the morning. So I ran and ran, all the way to the gates of the town, and got there just as the last soldiers were going inside. I look, and who do I see? I see Cornet Galjandowicz!* He is an old acquaintance of mine—for three years now he's owed me a hundred gold ducats. So I run after him like I want to settle accounts, and that's how I managed to get into the town!"

"Well, would you believe it! So you got inside and wanted to get back what he owed you on top of it!" Bulba said. "I'm surprised he didn't have you hanged like a dog!"

---

* A cornet was a cavalry officer.

"As God is my witness, he did want to have me hanged!" the Jew replied. "His servants had already grabbed hold of me and tied a noose around my neck, but I fell on my knees before him and swore I would wait as long as he wanted to get my money back. I even offered to lend him more if he promised to help me collect the money the other knights owed me—for you see, Cornet Galjandowicz doesn't have as much as a brass coin in his pocket! Even though he has farms, estates, four castles, and owns the steppes all the way to Shklov, when it comes to ready money he's just like a Cossack—he hasn't got a groshen to his name!* If the Breslau Jews hadn't kitted him out with armor he'd have had to march to war with nothing on his back. That's why he's never shown his face at the Parliament Council, and never—"

"What did you do inside the town? Did you see any of our men?"

"Of course I did! There's lots of our men there: Itzik, Rakhum, Samuel, Haivaloh our Jew pawnbroker—"

"To hell with those dogs!" Taras yelled in a rage. "What do I care about your damn Jewish cronies! I'm asking you about our Zaporozhian men!"

"I didn't see any of our Zaporozhians, I only saw Master Andri."

"You saw Andri!" Bulba shouted. "What do you mean? Where did you see him? In a cellar? A pit? Defiled? Tied up?"

"Tied up? Who would dare tie up Master Andri? He is such a grand knight now. . . . As God is my witness, I barely recognized him! His shoulder straps are golden, his sleeve cuffs are golden, his breastplate's golden, his hat's golden, his belt's golden—gold everywhere, all over! He sparkles with gold like the sun in spring, when all the little birdies are in the garden twittering and the grasses smell all nice. And the governor even gave him his best horse—worth at least two hundred gold ducats!"

Bulba froze. "But why would he be wearing foreign armor?"

---

* Groshen: the smallest denomination of Polish coin.

"Because it's better, that's why! And he rides about, and the others ride about. He teaches them things, they teach him things. He's like the richest Polish nobleman!"

"Who could have forced him to do this?"

"I wouldn't say anyone forced him to do anything. Didn't you know he went over to them by his own free will?"

"Who went over to them?"

"Master Andri."

"Went over where?"

"Went over to their side! He's one of them now."

"You are lying, you pig's rump!"

"Why would I be lying? Am I a fool to be lying? Would I stick out my own head with such a lie? Do you think I don't know that a Jew is hanged the minute he tells a Cossack even the smallest little lie?"

"So what you are saying is, according to you, that Andri has betrayed faith and fatherland?"

"I'm not saying he has betrayed anything. I'm just saying he went over to the Poles."

"These are lies, you damn Jew! Lies, the like of which have never been heard in all Christendom! You're wrong, you dog!"

"May grass grow over the threshold of my house if I'm wrong! May every man, woman, and child spit on the graves of my father, my mother, my father-in-law, my father's father, and my mother's father if I am wrong! If you want, I'll even tell you why he went over to them!"

"Why?"

"The governor has a beautiful daughter. Holy God, what a beauty!" The Jew tried as hard as he could to convey her beauty, stretching his arms out wide, narrowing his eyes into a squint, and puckering his lips as if he were about to taste a most delicate morsel.

"What's that got to do with it?"

"It is for her that he's done this. He went over to them because of her. When a man falls in love, he becomes like the waterlogged sole of a shoe—you can bend it any way you want."

Taras Bulba thought hard. He remembered the great power the weakest of women had, how some of the strongest men had been driven to ruin, and how pliable Andri's nature was in this respect. For a long time he stood rooted to the spot.

"Listen, I'll tell you everything," Yankel said. "When I heard the noise and saw the troops marching to the town gates, I said to myself, 'You never know,' and took along a string of pearls, as there are beautiful women and women of the nobility in the town, and I said to myself, 'They might have nothing to eat, but I bet you they'll buy pearls!' And the minute the cornet's servants let me go, I ran to the governor's house to sell the pearls, and there was a Tatar maidservant there who told me there was to be a wedding the moment the Zaporozhians were chased away, and that Master Andri had promised to chase them away."

"And you didn't kill that devil's cur then and there?" Bulba shouted.

"Why kill him? He went of his own free will. It's better there for him, he went there—you can't blame a man for that!"

"And you saw him with your own eyes?"

"With my very eyes, by God! What a glorious warrior! The handsomest of them all! May God give him health! He recognized me immediately, and when I went up to him, he said to me right away—"

"What did he say?"

"He said . . . Well, first he motioned me with his finger, and then he said, 'Yankel,' he said, and I said, 'Master Andri!' and he said, 'Yankel, tell my father and tell my brother, tell the Cossacks and tell the Zaporozhians, tell everyone that my father is no longer my father, my brother no longer my brother, my comrades no longer my comrades, and that I will fight them all. All of them I'll fight!'"

"You are lying, you devilish Judas!" Taras yelled in a frenzy. "You are lying, you dog! It was you who nailed Jesus to the Cross, you fiend cursed by God! I shall kill you, Satan!" Taras shouted, unsheathing his saber. "Get out of my sight or I'll kill you here and now!"

The frightened Jew ran off as fast as his thin, spindly legs could carry him. Without looking back he ran the whole length of the Cossack camp and far over the open fields, even though Taras was not chasing him. Taras had decided that there was no sense in taking his fury out on the first man he could grab hold of.

Taras suddenly remembered seeing Andri walking through the camp with a woman the night before, and he lowered his gray head, though he still could not believe that such a heinous thing could have come to pass, that his own son had betrayed his faith and his soul. Finally he prepared his regiment for the ambush, hiding himself with his men in the only forest the Cossacks had not burnt, while the other Zaporozhians, both foot soldiers and horsemen, headed for the three roads that led to the town's three gates, gathering in their companies—Uman, Popovichev, Kanev, Steblikiv, Nezamaikov, Gurguziv, Titarev, and Timoshev. Only the Pereyaslav Company no longer existed. Its Cossacks had caroused so wildly that they had caroused their lives away. Some of them woke up with their arms and legs bound by enemy ropes; others did not wake up at all, entering the damp earth in their sleep; and Captain Khlib woke up in the Polish camp without his armor or his trousers.

The townsfolk heard the Cossacks regrouping, and gathered on the rampart, a magnificent sight: Polish knights lined up, each handsomer than the other, their burnished helmets shining like suns and bearing white, swanlike plumes. Others wore light hats, pink and blue in color with long tops folded to the side, and caftans with gold-embroidered doubled-back sleeves with delicate trimmings; they carried gem-studded sabers and muskets for which much money had been paid. There was finery everywhere. The colonel from Budzhaki, in a red and gold hat, stood pompously in front. He was a stout man, taller and fatter than the others, and his elaborate wide caftan barely managed to gird his frame. Some distance along the wall, almost by the side gate, stood another colonel, a short, gaunt man, his small sharp eyes flashing energetically from beneath thick, bushy brows. He turned quickly from side to side, briskly pointing his bony hand in all directions as he barked orders. It was clear that notwithstanding his small body he was a master military tactician. Near him stood the cornet, a lanky man with a full mustache and an abundantly crimson face. It was plain to see that he enjoyed a cup or two of strong mead and a good night of carousing. Behind them stood a full array of Polish noblemen in armor bought with their own ducats, or ducats from the King's treasury, or with ducats borrowed from Jews, pawning anything and everything they could find in their fathers' castles. There were also many hangers-on, whom senators took to banquets as a retinue and who stole silver spoons from tables, and then the following day climbed back onto their coach boxes in livery. There were men of every sort, men who might not have money for a dram of vodka but were nevertheless decked out in full splendor.

The Cossack ranks stood silently in front of the town walls. There was no trace of gold in their array, and only the glint of a weapon flashed from time to time from their lines. The Cossacks did not like a show of wealth in battle. They wore simple tunics and chain mail, and their black crimson-topped lambskin hats shone from afar with a dark red shimmer.

Two Cossacks rode forward from the Zaporozhian lines. One, Okhrim Nash, was quite young, the other, Mikita Golokopitenko, was a little older, but both were loudmouthed and good fighters in battle. They were followed by Demid Popovich, a robust Cossack who had been at the Sech for years. He had fought at Adrianople, and had been through much in his life. They had tried to burn him at the stake, but he had managed to escape to the Sech, his head blackened and his mustache singed. Popovich had recovered, his forelock had begun to grow back, and his thick mustache resprouted, black as coal. He had a very caustic mouth.

"What pretty tunics you are all wearing," he shouted up at the Poles. "But is your strength as pretty?"

"Just wait!" the hefty colonel shouted down from the wall. "I'll bind and gag you all! Hand over your weapons and your horses, you ruffians! Did you see your comrades with their arms and legs bound? Bring out the Cossack prisoners!" And the Cossacks, tied with ropes, were led out onto the ramparts, Captain Khlib in front, without his armor and trousers, just as he had been captured in his drunken stupor. The captain stared at his feet, ashamed in front of his Cossack comrades at his nakedness and having been captured in his sleep like a dog. His powerful head had turned gray in a single night.

"Cheer up, Khlib, we'll free you soon enough!" the Cossacks shouted from below.

"Yes, cheer up, brother!" Captain Borodaty called from his company. "You are not to blame that they captured you naked! Misfortune can befall any man! Shame upon those who are parading you like this without covering your nakedness!"

"I see that you Poles are the most valiant of warriors when fighting sleeping men!" Golokopitenko shouted from beneath the rampart.

"Wait till we shear off those Cossack forelocks of yours!" the Poles shouted back.

"I would love to see you try!" Popovich yelled, turning his horse to face the Poles, and then, looking back toward his men, added, "But you know, these Poles might be right after all! If that fat man up there will lead them out, then they might well have the best defense tactic in the world!"

"Why might they have the best defense tactic in the world?" another Cossack called out, confident that Popovich already had a good retort at his fingertips.

"Because he's so fat that their whole damn army can hide behind him! We'll be lucky if we can get past that big paunch of his to root out even one of those bastards!"

The Cossacks guffawed. Many shook their heads and said, "That Popovich! When he aims his tongue at a man, then . . ." But the Cossacks did not say what happened when Popovich aimed his tongue at a man.

"Away, away from the walls!" the Ataman shouted to the Cossacks, for the Poles were infuriated by the caustic words, and their colonel had waved them forward with his hand. The Cossacks had barely stepped back when grapeshot came showering down on them from the rampart. Commotion followed among the Poles, even the gray-haired governor appearing on his horse. The gates flew open, and the Polish army came pouring out. The Hussars rode in front in orderly formation, followed by foot soldiers in chain mail, armored spear carriers, and all the men in burnished helmets. After them the highest noblemen rode out one by one, each garbed in his own colors. The noblemen took pains to distance themselves from the rows of common soldiers, and those who did not have a brigade of their own rode out with their servants. More lines of foot soldiers followed, behind them the cornet. Then came more lines, followed by the fat colonel. The last to ride out was the spindly little colonel.

"Don't let them get into formation!" the Ataman shouted. "All companies attack now! Withdraw from the other gates! Titarev Company, attack from this side! Dyadkiv Company, attack from there! Kukubenko and Palivoda, attack the rear! Disperse them, break them up!"

The Cossacks attacked from all sides, hammering the Poles, throwing them into confusion and falling into confusion themselves. The Poles were not able to set up their muskets, so the battle was fought with sabers and lances. The Cossacks fought elbow to elbow, each man eager to show his prowess. Demid Popovich impaled three foot soldiers, and managed to knock two of the grandest noblemen from their mounts. "Fine horses!" he shouted. "Just the kind I need!" He sent the horses galloping out into the fields, calling out to the Cossacks there to catch them. He fought his way back into the throng, slaughtered one of the noblemen he had pulled off his mount, threw a noose around the other one's neck, tied it to his saddle, and dragged him across the field, after taking his gem-studded saber and snatching the pouch of gold ducats from his belt. Kobita, a brave Cossack and still a young man, confronted one of the most valiant warriors of the Polish army. They fought for a long time, finally fighting hand to hand. The Pole managed to gain the advantage, but as Kobita fell he plunged his Turkish dagger into the Pole's chest. But Fate did not spare Kobita either, and a burning bullet pierced his temple. The grandest among the Polish knights, a man of magnificent and princely lineage, had shot Kobita and then ridden off in cool elegance on his dun-colored steed. This Pole had already shown much valor and daring. He had slashed two Zaporozhians in half, and had knocked Fyodor Korzh, a fine Cossack, from his horse, shot the horse, and then with his lance speared Fyodor as he lay trapped beneath the animal. The Polish knight had already severed many Cossack heads and arms before he shot a bullet into young Kobita's temple.

"There's a warrior I'd like to match my strength with!" yelled Kukubenko, captain of the Nezamaikov Company, and, spurring his horse, he rode at him from behind with a deafening and inhuman cry that sent shudders down the spines of all the men nearby. The Polish knight tried to turn his horse around to face Kukubenko, but the horse balked, startled by the terrible cry, veered to the side, and Kukubenko toppled the knight from his mount, hitting him with a burning bullet between the shoulder blades. The knight did not yield. He fought back, but his arm began to weaken. Kukubenko raised his heavy broadsword and drove it between the Pole's ashen lips, knocking out two milk-white teeth, cutting his tongue in half, piercing the bones of his neck, and plunging deep into the soil, nailing the knight forever to the damp earth. A fountain of noble crimson blood gushed forth, blossoming out like a spray of wild riverside roses, reddening the knight's yellow gold-embroidered caftan. But Kukubenko and his men were already hacking away at another swarm of Poles.

"I can't believe Kukubenko left such precious armor lying there!" Borodaty mumbled, and left his Uman Company, riding over to where the slaughtered nobleman lay. "I've cut down seven Poles, but none had armor like this!" Borodaty was beguiled by greed. He knelt down to remove the Pole's costly armor, took a gem-studded Turkish dagger, untied a bag of gold ducats from the dead man's belt, took from his chest a bag with fine undergarments, precious silver, and a girl's lock of hair kept as a memento. He did not hear rushing at him from behind the red-nosed cornet, whom he had already thrown off his mount once and given a good slash to remember him by. The cornet swung his sword with all his might, bringing it down on Borodaty's neck. Greed was the Cossack's undoing. His powerful head skidded off his shoulders, and his headless body fell, a violent spray of blood drenching the earth all around, his rough Cossack soul rising to the heavens, railing with fury, but also taken aback that it had to leave such a strong body so early. The cornet did not have time to grab the severed head by its forelock and tie it to his saddle, for a grim avenger appeared like a hawk flying wide circles high in the sky, its power-ful wings spread wide, stopping suddenly before plummeting like an arrow at the quail squealing in terror. That is how Ostap, Taras Bulba's son, suddenly came flying at the cornet. Ostap threw a rope around his neck, the cornet's red face growing even redder as the cruel noose gar-roted him. The cornet grabbed his pistol, but his raised arm shook convulsively and he fired the bullet out into the field. Ostap undid the silk rope that the cornet had knotted to his saddle for tying up prison-ers, bound his arms and legs, attached the end to his saddle, and dragged the cornet across the field. Ostap called out to the Cossacks of the Uman Company that their captain had just been killed, and the men immediately left the fray and hurried to collect his body, confer-ring with one another as to whom they should choose as their new captain. "Why even discuss the matter? The best man to choose is Bulba's son Ostap! He is younger than all of us, but he has the wisdom of an old man!"

Ostap took off his hat and thanked his Cossack comrades for the honor they were conferring on him. He did not, as modesty required, argue against his election, aware that a battlefield was no place for formalities, and so he immediately led the Uman Company back into the fray, where it soon became clear that the men had chosen wisely.

The Poles began to feel that the situation was becoming too dangerous for them, and they ran across the field to regroup at the other end. The spindly colonel waved to a battalion of four hundred that was positioned near the town's gate, and volleys of grapeshot came thundering into the Cossack swarm. But this did not have the expected effect. The bullets hit the Cossacks' oxen, which were watching the battle with terror in their eyes, and the frightened beasts roared and turned in a stampede back toward the Cossack camp, smashing carts and trampling many men. But Taras and his regiment immediately broke away from their position of ambush, and faced the stampede with loud yells. The crazed animals, terrified by the shouts, turned back and charged at the Poles, knocking the horsemen off their mounts and throwing the formations into disarray.

"Thank you, dear oxen!" the Zaporozhians shouted. "You have already proven yourselves on our long march, and now you have proven yourselves in battle, too!" And the Cossacks threw themselves at the enemy with renewed vigor. They slaughtered a great number of Poles. Many Cossacks distinguished themselves in battle—Metelitsa, Shilo, both Pisarenkos, Vovtuzenko. The Poles, seeing that things were going badly for them, turned their battle standards around and yelled for the town gates to be opened. The heavy iron gates opened with a loud rasp to receive the exhausted, mud-spattered horsemen, who came thronging in like sheep into a pen. Many of the Cossacks chased after them, but Ostap stopped his men, shouting, "Away from the walls, away from the walls! Don't get too close!"

And he was right, because the townsfolk began hurling down from the walls whatever they could get their hands on, and many Cossacks were struck.

"We have a new captain who leads his company like an old hand!" the Ataman called out, riding up to Ostap. Taras Bulba turned to see who this new captain might be, and saw Ostap riding in front of the Uman Company, wielding a captain's baton, his hat cocked to the side.

"Well!" Bulba said, looking at him with joy and thanking the Uman men for the honor they had accorded his son.

The Cossacks retreated and began heading to their camps. The Poles had assembled on the ramparts once more, this time with their elegant garb in tatters. Many of their costly caftans were caked with blood, and the beautiful burnished helmets were covered in mud.

"So you captured us and tied us up, did you?" the Cossacks shouted up to the Poles.

"We will, just you wait!" the fat colonel yelled back from the rampart, waving a rope at them.

The soldiers, exhausted and covered in mud, continued shouting threats, the most vigorous men on both sides vying to outshout one another. But finally the Cossacks dispersed. Many of them, exhausted by the battle, lay down to rest, while others sprinkled soil over their wounds and tore into shreds for bandages the precious scarves and tunics they had taken from the killed enemy. The men who felt strong enough set out to collect the dead bodies of their comrades in order to bury them with honors. They dug graves using their broadswords and lances and removed the earth in their hats and tunics. They laid out the Cossack bodies and covered them with fresh earth so that rapacious ravens and eagles would not peck out their eyes. They tied the bodies of the Polish slain in dozens to the tails of wild horses, whipping and chasing the animals far out onto the steppes, the crazed horses dragging the mud-caked, blood-drenched corpses behind them as they galloped over furrows and knolls and through hollows and streams.

The companies sat in circles to eat their evening meal, and late into the night the men spoke of their feats in battle, feats that would be remembered by generations of Cossacks to come. Taras Bulba also stayed awake till the early hours, wondering why Andri had not appeared among the enemy warriors. Was that Judas ashamed of marching against his own people, or had the Jew been lying and Andri taken prisoner after all? And yet Taras remembered how easily Andri's heart could falter at a beautiful woman's words, and felt grief, swearing grim vengeance against the Polish woman who had bewitched his son. He was resolved to carry out his oath. He would grab her magnificent thick hair without a single glance at her beauty and drag her over the field through the rows of Cossacks, her exquisite breasts and shoulders that had sparkled like the eternal snows on the highest peaks skidding over the ground and covered in grime and blood. He would rip her beautiful limbs to pieces. But Bulba did not know what God had in store for the following day, and, sinking into dreams, he finally fell asleep.

The Cossacks continued to talk among themselves, and all night the clear-eyed watch stood by the fires, looking steadily in all directions.

8

The sun had not yet reached the middle of the sky when all the Zaporozhians gathered into a circle. Word had come that during their absence the Tatars had raided the Sech, dug up the treasures the Cossacks had hidden, slaughtered or taken captive all who had remained behind, and set out to Perekop with the herds of horses and cattle they had rounded up. A single Cossack, Maksim Golodukha, had managed to escape. He had stabbed the Tatar chieftain, untied his sack of gold ducats, and in Tatar garb and on a Tatar steed had ridden two days and two nights, dodging his pursuers. He had ridden his horse to death, had mounted another horse, which he also rode to death, and on the third horse arrived at the Cossack camp that was besieging Dubno. He managed to tell the Cossacks the terrible news, but was too exhausted to explain how the evil had come about, whether the Cossacks who had remained at the Sech had been carousing as Cossacks do and consequently been captured drunk. Nor did he say how it was that the Tatars had found out where the treasure of the Sech was buried. Golodukha was too exhausted to speak further, his body bloated by fatigue, his face burnt by the sun and scorched by the wind. He sank to the ground and instantly fell asleep.

When marauders raided the Sech, the Cossacks always charged after them right away in an effort to catch up with them, as the captives were usually sold in the bazaars of Asia Minor, Smyrna, and the island of Crete, and God knew where else the forelocked heads of the Zaporozhians might end up. This was why the Zaporozhians had now gathered in a circle. All the men kept their hats on, because they had not gathered to hear the Ataman's orders but to confer as equals with one another.

"Let the elders first give us counsel!" some of the men shouted.

"Let the Ataman give us counsel!" others shouted.

The Ataman took off his hat, in the manner of a comrade and not as a chief, and thanked the Cossacks for the honor. "Many among us are older and wiser than I in counsel," he said, "but as you have honored me, my counsel is that we should hunt down the Tatars right away. We all know what kind of men they are. They will not wait around with the plunder until we arrive, but will see to it that nothing remains. So my counsel is that we go after them! We have already had our fun here. We have taught the Poles who the Cossacks are, and we have avenged our faith as well as we could. And furthermore, we cannot expect great spoils in a starving town. So my counsel is: We must go after the Tatars!"

"We must go after the Tatars!" voices exploded from all the Zaporozhian companies.

But these words were not to Taras Bulba's liking, and he lowered his sullen white eyebrows, which were streaked with black like the thicket that grows on dark mountains whose peaks the north wind covers with biting hoarfrost. "No, your counsel is wrong, Ataman!" he said. "What you are saying is wrong! Have you forgotten that there are men of ours still being held prisoner by the Poles? We must honor the first holy law of brotherhood—we cannot leave our brothers to be skinned alive, drawn and quartered, and their corpses paraded through villages and towns, as was done with our Hetman and the greatest heroes of the Ukraine. Have these Poles not defiled our churches enough? I ask you all: What are we? What kind of Cossack is he who pushes away a comrade in need, flings him off like a dog to perish on foreign soil? If things have come to the point that we no longer defend Cossack honor and look the other way when men hurl offending words at our elders and spit on their gray beards, then I will be glad to stay back here alone!"

The Cossacks began to be swayed.

"But have you forgotten, Colonel Bulba, that we also have comrades in Tatar hands?" the Ataman said. "If we don't hasten to free them, they will be forced to live in eternal slavery under the heathens—a fate worse than the cruelest death! Have you forgotten that these Tatars have seized all the treasures for which we spilled our Christian blood?"

The Cossacks were confounded, and did not know what to say. No one wanted to open his mouth and end up earning a shameful reputation. Then Kasan Bovdyug, the oldest warrior in all the Zaporozhian army, stepped forward. The Cossacks held him in high honor. He had been elected Ataman twice and had proven himself a strong fighter in the wars, but he had grown old and had not taken part in any of the campaigns for a long time. He also did not like giving advice to anybody, but preferred making himself comfortable in Cossack gatherings and listening to tales of past feats. He never voiced his opinion when the other Cossacks spoke, but simply listened, pressing down with the tip of his finger the ashes in the little pipe that he never removed from his mouth, and sat there motionless, narrowing his eyes. The Cossacks never knew whether he had dozed off or was still listening. He no longer rode into battle, but this time the old man had not been able to resist coming along. He had waved his hands in Cossack fashion and said, "The devil take it, I'm coming along! Who knows, I might still be able to be of some service to the Cossack cause!"

All the Cossacks fell silent when Bovdyug stepped out in front of the gathering, as no one remembered having heard him say a single word for a very long time. Every man wanted to know what Kasan Bovdyug was going to say.

"My turn has come to speak, brothers!" he began. "Listen to the words of an old man! The Ataman spoke wisely, and as he is the head of the Cossack army it is his duty to safeguard it and to safeguard its treasure. He could not have spoken words more wise! That is the first thing I wanted to say. And now listen to the second thing I want to say: Colonel Bulba also spoke very true words—may God grant him a long life and the Ukraine many more colonels like him! The foremost duty and honor of every Cossack is to defend the Cossack spirit. In all my long life, brothers, I have never heard of a Cossack abandoning or betraying a comrade. Both the prisoners here and the men taken prisoner by the Tatars are our comrades. Whether there are more of them here or less there is not the question. They are all comrades, and all are dear to us! So this is what I have to say: Those closest to the men taken captive by the Tatars, let them set out against the Tatars, and those closest to the men taken captive by the Poles and who do not want to leave this just cause unfinished, let them stay. The Ataman, as is his duty, will lead the half who will march against the Tatars, and the other half will elect a provisional Ataman. As for the provisional Ataman: If you wish to listen to the words of a white-haired old man, then the provisional Ataman should be Taras Bulba. There is no man among us who can stand up to him in valor!"

Kasan Bovdyug fell silent, and the Cossacks rejoiced that the old man had made them see reason. "We thank you!" they shouted, throwing their hats in the air. "You have been silent so long, so very long, but in the end, when you did speak, yours were the truest words! When we set out on this campaign you said that you might be of use to the Cossack cause, and you were right!"

"Do you all agree?" the Ataman asked.

"We all agree!" the Cossacks shouted.

"The assembly has ended?"

"The assembly has ended!" the Cossacks shouted.

"Listen to my military order, brothers!" the Ataman said, stepping forward and putting on his hat, and all the Cossacks removed their hats and stood with uncovered heads, lowering their eyes as has always been the Cossack custom when the Ataman is about to speak.

"You must split into two groups! All those who want to go, step to the right, and those who want to stay, step to the left. To whatever side the larger part of a company goes is the side to which that company's captain must go too. Wherever only a small part of a company is left, those men must join other companies."

The men began to gather on either side. Whenever the largest part of a company assembled on one side, its captain followed, and the remaining men joined other companies, and it turned out that there was more or less the same number of men on either side. The Uman and Kanev Companies had decided to stay, as had almost the whole of the Nezamaikov Company, and the larger part of the Popovichev, the Steblikiv, and the Timoshev companies. The rest resolved to pursue the Tatars. There were many brave and robust Cossacks on both sides. Among those who decided to hunt down the Tatars were Cherevati, a worthy old Cossack, Pokotipole, Lemish, and Prokopovich Khoma. Demid Popovich also decided to go, because he had an extremely unbridled nature and could not bear staying in one place for too long. He had already taken on the Poles and now wanted to take on the Tatars. The captains were Nostyugan, Pokrishka, and Nevilichky. Many more brave and glorious Cossacks wanted to try their swords and fists in combat with the Tatars. There were also many good and strong Cossacks who decided to stay: Captains Demitrovich, Kukubenko, Vertikhvist, Balaban, and Ostap Bulbenko, and the valiant Cossacks Vovtuzenko, Cherevichenko, Stepan Guska, Okhrim Guska, Mikola Gusty, Zadorozhny, Metelitsa, Ivan Zakrutiguba, Mosei Shilo, Dyegtarenko, Sidorenko, and the three Pisarenkos. On foot and on horseback they had marched down the coast of Anatolia, across the Crimean salt fields and steppes, along the big and small rivers that pour into the Dnieper, and all the bays and islands of the Dnieper. They had also been to Moldavian, Walachian, and Turkish lands. They had traveled the Black Sea in double-ruddered Cossack skiffs, fifty skiffs in a row attacking the wealthiest and grandest ships; they had sunk quite a number of Turkish galleys and had fired a great amount of gunpowder. Many times they had ripped precious silks and velvets into foot wrappings and stuffed the moneybags hanging on their belts with gold ducats. And the wealth each of them had drunk and caroused away was more than could be summed up, and was more than enough to support a man all his life. They had squandered everything in Cossack fashion, plying friends and strangers with vodka and hiring crowds of musicians to carouse wildly with them. And yet there was hardly one of them who didn't have treasures buried beneath the reeds of the Dnieper islands—tankards, silver cups, bracelets—this so that the Tatars would not find anything, if by great misfortune they ever managed to take the Sech by surprise. But it would be hard enough for the Tatars to find the treasure, as the Cossacks themselves often could not remember where they had buried things. These were the Cossacks who wanted to remain and seek vengeance from the Poles for their comrades and the True Faith. Old Bovdyug also wanted to stay with them. "I'm not at an age to go chasing after Tatars, and this is the right kind of place for a good Cossack death. For a long time now I have begged God that, when my time came to die, I would meet death on the battlefield fighting for the true Christian faith. And God has granted my wish, for where can an old Cossack find a more glorious death than here?"

When all had gathered into two groups of companies, the Ataman walked through the ranks. "Brothers, are both sides happy with their choice?" he asked.

"We are happy with our choice!" the Cossacks answered.

"In that case, kiss and say farewell, for God knows if you will see one another again in this life. Listen to your Ataman! You know what you must do, you know what Cossack honor demands!"

And all the Cossacks kissed one another—first the company captains kissed three times, and then took hold of each other's hands and clasped them tightly.* The men wanted to ask one another, "Will we see each other again, brother, or will we never see each other again?" But they remained silent, and lowered their gray heads. They bade farewell, knowing that much travail lay ahead for both groups. They decided not to separate right away but to wait for darkness to set in, so that the Poles would not notice the weakening of their forces. Then all the companies set out for their camps to eat a noonday meal.

After they had eaten, the Cossacks who were to set out lay down to rest and fell into a long and deep sleep, almost as if this might be their last sleep in freedom. They slept until sundown. With the first twilight, they began tarring the wheels of their carts. When they finished their preparations, they set their carts rolling and, waving their hats in farewell, silently walked behind them. The cavalry sedately followed the infantry in a light trot, without shouting or whistling at their horses, and soon they, too, disappeared into the darkness. There was only the dull thud of horses' hooves and the occasional squeak of a wheel that had not been tarred well enough in the darkness.

The Cossacks who stayed behind stood and waved for a long time, even though nothing could be seen in the dark. They returned to their camps, and when they saw by the bright starlight that half the carts were no longer there and that so many of their comrades had left, their hearts grew heavy; they became dejected, and let their heads sink.

Taras saw how dispirited his men were, and how dejection unworthy of valiant Cossacks had begun to seep silently into their heads. But he said nothing. He wanted to give them time to get used to the new arrangement and also to the dejection brought about by their com-

---

* To kiss three times was a manifestation of friendship symbolizing the Holy Trinity.

rades' departure. He thought of a way to shake them out of their stupor in whooping Cossack fashion so that their good spirits would come back even stronger than before, as only the spirits of the Slavic race can—that broad and sweeping race that is to other races what the ocean is to trickling streams. When a storm rages this ocean roars and thunders with mountainous waves the like of which no stream has ever seen, and when the storm has passed, this same ocean stretches in a boundless, crystalline expanse.

Taras Bulba ordered his servants to unload one of his carts that stood apart from the others and was larger and more solid than the rest. Its sturdy wheels were carefully wrapped; its heavy load was covered with horse blankets and strong ox hides and tied down with heavily tarred ropes. On the cart were flasks and kegs of precious wine that had aged for years in Taras's cellars. He had brought the wine along for a celebration, so that if there were momentous feats worthy of passing on to future generations, then all the Cossacks would drink the rare wine to celebrate. Taras Bulba's servants rushed to the cart and cut the strong ropes with their broadswords, raised the heavy ox hides and horse blankets, and unloaded the flasks and kegs.

"All of you come here!" Bulba shouted to the Cossacks. "Each and every one of you, grab whatever you can lay your hands on—ladles, gloves, hats, the buckets you water your horses with—or just cup your hands together!"

And the Cossacks held out ladles, gloves, hats, or the buckets with which they watered their horses, or just cupped their hands together, while Taras's servants walked along the rows pouring wine from the flasks and kegs. The men were not to drink until Taras gave the order, as he wanted them all to drink at the same time. He also wanted to make a speech, for he knew that no matter how potent the fine wine was, and how capable of strengthening a man's soul, if one added a word or two, then the wine and the soul ended up twice as strong.

"I am inviting you to drink, brothers, not in honor of your making me your Ataman—great though this honor is—and not in honor of the comrades who have just left!" Bulba began. "In other times, such occasions would be cause for celebration, but this is not a time for celebration! We have before us a feat of great toil, of great Cossack valor. And so comrades, we will drink first and foremost to the holy Russian Orthodox faith: may the time come that it will spread over the whole earth, so that there be a single True Faith everywhere, and that every last Polish heathen, every last one, becomes a true Christian! And we will also drink to the Sech, that it may triumph in the destruction of the heathen faith, and that every year the Sech will produce one man better than the other, one man handsomer than the other. Let us all drink to our own glory so that our grandsons and their sons can someday say that once there were men who did not bring shame to the Cossack cause and did not betray their own. To the True Faith, brothers! To the True Faith!"

"To the True Faith!" the men roared in the rows nearest to Taras Bulba.

"To the True Faith!" echoed the men farther back, and young and old drank to it.

"To the Sech!" Taras Bulba shouted, raising his cup high above his head.

"To the Sech!" the first rows thundered.

"To the Sech!" the old men said quietly, their gray mustaches quivering. And the young men ruffling themselves up like falcons shouted: "To the Sech!" The wide field heard the Cossacks honor their Sech.

"The final drop, comrades—to glory and to all the Christians on earth!" And the Cossacks drank to glory and to all the Christians on earth.

The buckets and ladles were empty, but the Cossacks still stood with raised arms. Though the wine had given all their eyes a cheerful sparkle, the men were still dejected. They were not thinking of profit and the spoils of war, nor about who would be lucky enough to get their hands on gold ducats, precious weapons, embroidered caftans, or Circassian horses. But they brooded like eagles perched on jagged mountain peaks, peering into the distance over a boundless sea sprinkled with boats and galleys, and hemmed by a blurry coastline with little towns clustering like flies and forests swaying like delicate grass. The Cossacks peered like eagles across the field at their destiny shimmering darkly in the distance, the whole terrain with its hillocks and paths strewn with their white bones jutting up from the grass, heaped with shattered carts and broken sabers and spears, and drenched with their Cossack blood. Cossack heads with bloody tangled forelocks and mustaches were scattered wide over the field, eagles hacking and ripping out Cossack eyes. But there is good in a camp over which death stretches so wide and free. Not a single valiant deed will be lost, and Cossack glory will not be puffed away like a speck of gunpowder from the muzzle of a musket. There will be a bandura player with a gray beard hanging down to his chest who will sing of the valiant deeds, or perhaps a white-haired old man still filled with ripe vigor, who can see into men's souls and who will speak of these Cossacks in powerful and exalted words. And the Cossacks' glory will spread proudly, galloping to the ends of the earth, and generations to come will speak of these valiant men. For powerful words echo far, like the thunder of an illustrious bell into which a master has melded precious silver so that the sound will carry far over towns and villages, huts and palaces, calling all to holy prayer.

9

Nobody in the town realized that half the Zaporozhian army had left to pursue the Tatars. The watchmen on the tower of the town hall saw a number of carts retreating into the forest, but they thought the Cossacks were preparing some sort of ambush. A French engineer stationed in the town was under the same impression. The Ataman had predicted that there would be a lack of provisions among the Poles, and he was right: in those days armies did not calculate the amount of supplies they might need. The Poles attempted a go-for-broke sortie, but half were slaughtered immediately and the other half were chased back into the town empty-handed. The Jews, however, turned the sortie to their advantage, getting wind of why half the Zaporozhian army was gone. They found out which captains and which companies had left, how many men had gone and how many had stayed behind, and what the Cossacks were planning.

The Poles had barely returned from their sortie when the whole town knew everything, and the colonels took heart and prepared an onslaught. By the movement and commotion that came from within the town, Taras Bulba immediately realized what they had in mind; he promptly took action, sending out instructions and orders and rallying his men. He split the companies into three camps and had the carts arranged around them like a fortress, a way of fighting in which the Cossacks were unmatched. He ordered two of the companies to prepare for an ambush: he covered part of the field with sharp spikes and shattered lances, as he intended to chase the enemy cavalry onto them. When everything was ready he made a speech to the Cossacks, not to rouse them, as they were already in high spirits, but merely to say what was in his heart.

"I want to tell you what our Cossack brotherhood is all about! You have heard your fathers and grandfathers speak of the high honor in which all men held our land! The Greeks knew who we were, Czargrad supplied us with gold ducats, and we had magnificent towns, and cathedrals, and princes—princes of Russian ancestry! Yes, we had our own princes, not Catholic heathens! But those heathens took all that away from us! We lost everything! We Zaporozhians were all that was left, we were left like an orphan or a widow who has lost a strong husband, and our native land was as orphaned as we were! It was in those days that we came together and clasped hands in brotherhood! That is what our brotherhood is! There is no holier tie! A father loves his children, a mother loves her children, and the children love their father and mother. But that is not all there is to it, brothers, for a beast loves its offspring, too! It is man alone who can bind himself to another through his soul and not merely through his blood. In other places there have also been brotherhoods, but there has never been a brotherhood such as we have here in Russia! Almost every one of you has traveled to foreign lands, and you have seen that there are men in foreign lands too, all created by God! You can talk with these men just as you can talk with one another. But the moment you try to speak a word from the heart, well, there you have it: yes, they might be clever men, yet they are different! They might be men just like you and me, yet they are different! No, brothers! To love as the Russian soul can love, not with the mind or whatever, but with everything that God has given us, with everything that is inside us—no, nobody else can love like that!" Taras said, waving his hands and shaking his gray head and mustache. "I know how badly things stand in our land. All that men think about is how many haystacks and herds of horses they have, and whether their mead is safely locked away in their cellars. They have taken on the devil knows what heathen habits. They loathe their own mother tongue, one man won't speak to another, men sell their own brothers as beasts are sold on market squares! The favor of the Polish King—and, often enough, not even the favor of the King but the cheap favor of a Polish magnate who will kick them in the face with his elegant boot—is dearer to these men than any brotherhood. But even the lowest scoundrel, the lowest of the low, though he may have scraped and bowed, rolled about groveling in the mud, even he, brothers, has a spark of Russian sentiment which can burst into flame! The poor wretch will pound his fists and clasp his head in his hands, cursing his worthless life, thirsting for any torture to atone for his shameful ways. And may all men know that this is what brotherhood means on Russian soil! And when the time comes to die, not a single one of them will manage to die as we will! Not a single one of them, for these wretches are mice, not men!"

Taras Bulba finished his speech, but continued shaking his head, which had grayed in so many Cossack campaigns. All the men were moved; his words had driven deep into their hearts. Even the oldest in the lines stood still, their gray heads hanging, tears trickling from their eyes, which they slowly wiped with their sleeves. And then, as if by a sign, they all threw up their arms and shook their grizzled heads. Taras had reminded them of what they already knew. Within the wartried fighters, he kindled the best that is in the hearts of men who have grown wise through sorrow, hardship, and every adversity of life, and his words also stirred the unharrowed souls of the younger men, the pride of the aged parents who had begotten them.

The enemy army poured out of the town, drums rolling and trumpets blaring, the noblemen riding in proud elegance, surrounded by numberless servants. The fat colonel shouted out orders. The Poles began advancing in tight rows toward the Cossack camps, yelling threats, aiming their weapons, flashing their eyes, and gleaming in their burnished armor. The instant the Cossacks saw that the Poles were within range, they began firing their muskets in unison in a constant barrage. The thundering shots carried far over the fields and meadows, melting into a ceaseless din and blanketing the battlefield in thick smoke. The Zaporozhians continued their incessant shooting, the men in the rear loading the muskets and passing them to the men in front, the enemy unable to grasp how the Cossacks managed to keep up their fire without having to stop to reload. By now the smoke had engulfed both armies and neither side could see anything anymore, nor could they tell how many men they had lost. But the Poles felt the torrent of bullets, and realized that their position was becoming perilous. They pulled back to get away from the smoke and regroup, and saw that many of their men had fallen. On the Cossack side, however, only two or three men in a hundred had been killed, and the Cossacks continued their ceaseless fire. Even the foreign engineer was amazed at this tactic, which he had never seen before. "These Cossacks are valiant men!" he told the Poles. "Armies in other lands would do well to adopt their methods!" And he suggested that the cannons be pointed directly at the Zaporozhian lines. The wide throats of the cast-iron cannons roared, and the earth shuddered far into the distance, and twice as much smoke rolled over the battlefield. In towns near and far the smell of gunpowder filled streets and squares. But the cannons had been aimed too high and the scorching cannonballs flew in wide arcs, roaring with deafening howls over the Cossacks' heads and tearing deep into the earth beyond the battlefield, driving through the black soil and hurling it high into the air. The French engineer clasped his head in dismay at the cannoneers' ineptness, and rushed to aim the cannons himself, despite the ceaseless onslaught of fiery Cossack bullets.

Taras Bulba immediately saw that the Nezamaikov and Steblikiv Companies were at risk. "Get out from behind your carts and onto your horses!" he yelled.

It would have been too late for the Cossacks had not Ostap plunged right to the enemy's heart, knocking the fuses out of the hands of six cannoneers, missing only four as the Poles came riding after him. The French engineer snatched up one of the fuses himself to set off a cannon that was bigger than any the Cossacks had ever seen, a thousand corpses grimly glaring at them through its gruesome mouth. It roared, and three cannons echoed its roar, the earth shaking in dull fourfold resonance. The cannon caused much havoc. Many aged mothers would beat their withered breasts with bony hands and bewail their fallen Cossack sons, and many women were widowed in Glukhov, Nemirov, Chernigov. Young women were to run through the bazaar every day, looking into every man's face to see if the one they loved had returned from war, and though over the years many armies would march through the town, the men these women loved would never be among them.

In a flash it was as if half the Nezamaikov Company had never existed. As a hailstorm flattens a field where every sheaf of wheat stands radiant as a gold ducat, the cannon flattened the men. The Cossacks now hurled themselves on the Poles in renewed fury. Captain Kukubenko flew into a rage when he saw that the greater part of his company had been wiped out. He and his remaining men threw themselves into the midst of the Poles, Kukubenko in his anger hacking to pieces the first Pole he came upon. He flung many cavalrymen from their horses, impaling both horse and horseman with his lance, and slashed his way through to the artillery line, where he captured one of the cannons. There he saw that the captain of the Uman Company had also pushed forward to the artillery line, and Stepan Guska was about to capture the main cannon. Leaving them to it, Kukubenko turned with his men to another horde of Poles. Wherever the Nezamaikov Company charged, a road opened up, and whenever the company turned, a side street cleared, the enemy lines lightening as the Poles fell in droves. Vovtuzenko was fighting by the carts, with Cherevichenko farther in front, while Dyegtarenko was fighting toward the back of the carts, with Captain Vertikhvist behind him. Dyegtarenko had already speared two Polish knights with his lance and was now attacking a third knight, who was strong, wore opulent armor, and had a retinue of fifty-one servants. The knight drove him back forcefully. He pushed Dyegtarenko to the ground, and, raising his saber, shouted, "There's not one among you Cossack dogs who would dare fight me!"

"I would dare fight you!" Mosei Shilo shouted, stepping forward. He was a muscular man who had often led the Cossacks in sea campaigns and had seen much hardship in his life. He and his men had been captured by the Turks at Trebizond and sent to work as slaves on the galleys, with arms and legs shackled. The Turks had let them starve for weeks on end, with nothing to drink but brackish seawater. The poor slaves had to endure countless ills for not renouncing their Christian faith. They held out, all but Captain Mosei Shilo. He trampled on Holy Writ and wound a foul turban on his sinful head. He managed to gain the confidence of the Pasha, and was made steward of the galley and foreman of the slaves. The poor slaves were very unhappy, for they knew that when a man betrays his faith and goes over to the oppressor, life under his yoke will be far more bitter than life under the yoke of a non-Christian. And that is how it was. Mosei Shilo made the men sit three in a row and had them shackled in new, stronger chains. He had them bound in ropes so tight they cut to the bone. He lashed their necks and backs. The Turks were overjoyed to have found such a servant, and when one day they forgot the Muslim law forbidding wine and drank themselves into a stupor, Shilo took all sixty-four keys and handed them to the slaves so they could free themselves, throw their chains and shackles into the sea, and cut the Turks' throats with their own sabers. The Cossacks gathered much plunder and returned glorious to the Sech, and for many years thereafter the bandura players sang of Shilo's feats. He would even have been elected Ataman, but he was an odd man. At times he performed deeds that the wisest among the elders could not have devised, and then sheer folly would get the better of him and he would drink and carouse everything away, amassing debts throughout the Sech; he would even steal like a common thief. One night he had taken a complete suit of armor and pawned it with the tavern keeper, for which he was tied to the post of shame in the bazaar with an oak cudgel placed next to him, so that every man who passed could give him a blow. But not a single man among all the Zaporozhians was prepared to lift the cudgel against him, for they all remembered his past achievements. That was the kind of Cossack Mosei Shilo was.

"Yes, there are men here ready to give you dogs a beating!" Shilo shouted, hurling himself at the Polish nobleman, and they began hacking at each other with their swords. Their breastplates and backplates were dented by the blows. The Pole cut through Shilo's chain mail, his blade ramming through to his body, turning his shirt red. But Shilo ignored the wound and slammed his heavy arm down onto the Pole's head, the burnished helmet flying off as he staggered and collapsed, with Shilo hacking and slashing at him. Let him be, Cossack, and turn around! But Shilo did not turn around. One of the dead man's servants slit his throat. Shilo turned to grab hold of the man, but the insolent Pole had already disappeared into the clouds of smoke. Shots were being fired from all sides. Shilo staggered and realized that he had been fatally wounded. He fell, laid his hand on his wound, and said to his comrades, "Farewell, brothers! Long live Orthodox Christian Russia, and may eternal honor be paid her!" He closed his weakening eyes, and his Cossack soul rose from his powerful body. At that moment Zadorozhny and his men came, and Captain Vertikhvist broke through the enemy lines, and also Balaban managed to advance.

"Brothers!" Taras called out to the captains. "Is there still gunpowder in our powder horns? Is our Cossack vigor going strong? Have the

Cossacks been brought to their knees?" At his words the Cossacks drove forward with even more vigor, throwing the enemy lines into utter confusion. The spindly Polish colonel signaled a gathering and ordered eight painted flags to be flown in order to muster all the Poles scattered over the field. They rushed toward the flags, but before they could gather in formation, Kukubenko and his Nezamaikov Company cut into their midst, Kukubenko hurling himself directly on the fat-bellied colonel. The colonel was no match for him and, turning his horse around, went galloping off. But Kukubenko chased him far into the field, not letting him rejoin his regiment. Stepan Guska saw them from his company, which was fighting on one of the flanks. He rode toward the colonel, lasso in hand, his head pressed against his horse's neck, and once he was in range, he flung the lasso around the colonel's neck. The colonel turned crimson and grabbed hold of the rope with both hands, struggling to tear it off, but with a hefty thrust a fatal spear was driven into his stomach. And there the fat colonel was to remain, pinned to the earth. But Stepan Guska fared no better. Before the Cossacks knew what was happening, they saw him impaled by four spears. "May all our enemies perish and our Russian lands triumph for all eternity!" he managed to gasp, and gave up his soul.

The Cossacks looked around and saw Metelitsa attacking the Poles on one side, cutting them down left and right, while Captain Nevilichky and his men advanced on the other side. Zakrutiguba was pushing the enemy back near the first line of carts, and toward the rear of the carts the youngest of the Pisarenkos was in pursuit of a whole swarm of Poles, while on top of the carts the men were already fighting hand to hand.

"Brothers!" Taras shouted, riding out in front of the others. "Do we still have gunpowder in our powder horns? Is our Cossack vigor holding up? Have the Cossacks been brought to their knees?"

"We still have powder in our powder horns!" the Cossacks called back. "Our Cossack vigor is holding up! The Cossacks have not been brought to their knees!"

Suddenly Bovdyug fell from one of the carts. A bullet had hit him right in the heart, but the old man gathered all his strength and said, "I am not saddened that I am leaving life. God grant every man an end like mine! Glory to the Russian lands for all eternity!" And his spirit rose to the heavens to relate to those long departed how men were fighting for Russia and were prepared to die for the Holy Faith.

Captain Balaban also fell soon after with three fatal wounds, from a spear, a bullet, and a heavy broadsword. He had been one of the most valiant Cossacks and had led many sea campaigns, but most glorious had been his campaign against the Anatolian shores. He and his men had brought back gold ducats, precious Turkish cloth, silks and velvets, and jewels of every kind, but they had run into misfortune on their way home, for they came under Turkish fire. Half their skiffs capsized and many men drowned, but the reed bundles tied to the sides stopped the skiffs from sinking. Balaban and his men rowed for all they were worth, heading straight into the line of the sun, making himself invisible to the Turkish ships. All night the Cossacks scooped out water with buckets and hats, and patched up all the cracks in their dugout skiffs. They cut their trousers into sails and set off, outsailing the fastest Turkish ship. Not only did they return to the Sech unscathed, but they also brought a gold-embroidered cassock for the Archimandrite of the Mezhigorsk Monastery in Kiev, and an icon setting of the purest silver for the Pokrov Church in Zaporozhe. For a long time after, the bandura players sang of their glorious feats.

Balaban lowered his head as he felt the pangs of death, and said quietly, "Brothers, I believe I am dying a good death. I cut down seven men, impaled nine with my lance, trampled many Poles with my horse, and I don't know how many I hit with my bullets. May Russia flourish forever!" And with these words his soul rose.

Cossacks, Cossacks! Do not offer up the most illustrious flower of your army! Kukubenko is surrounded—only seven men of the whole Nezamaikov Company are left, and they are fighting with their last strength. Kukubenko's tunic is covered in blood.

Taras Bulba, seeing Kukubenko's misfortune, rushed to help him, but he and his men came too late. Before the Poles who had surrounded Kukubenko could be driven off, they managed to plunge a lance into his heart. He sank into the arms of his Cossack comrades. His young blood gushed like a rare wine brought in a crystal decanter by a careless servant, who stumbles, breaking the precious carafe, the wine spilling onto the floor, the master tearing his hair, for this was the wine he had been saving for the most important occasion in his life, the day when by God's grace he met once more the beloved comrades of his youth to reminisce of bygone times when men knew how to revel. Kukubenko looked at his comrades and said, "I thank God that He has granted that I die among you. May the men who live after us be better men than we are, and may Russia, beloved by Christ, be forever triumphant!" And his young soul left his body to be raised by angels to heaven. He will be happy there. "Sit to my right, Kukubenko," Christ will say to him. "You did not betray the Cossack brotherhood, you never committed a dishonorable deed, you never abandoned a man in trouble, and you shielded and protected my church."

All the men were downcast by Kukubenko's death. The Cossack lines were weakening fast. Many courageous men were no longer among the living. But the Cossacks were still holding out.

"Brothers!" Taras called out to the remaining companies. "Is there still gunpowder in our powder horns? Are our sabers still sharp? Is our Cossack vigor going strong? Have the Cossacks been brought to their knees?"

"Our powder horns are full and our sabers are still sharp! Our Cossack vigor has not flagged, nor have the Cossacks been brought to their knees!"

The Cossacks hurled themselves into battle as if they had borne no losses. Only three captains were left alive. Red rivers, bridged by piles of dead Cossacks and Poles, were flowing everywhere. Taras looked up at the sky. A chain of vultures was approaching—they would feast.

Metelitsa was skewered by a Polish lance. The head of the second Pisarenko brother spun off his shoulders, eyes fluttering. Okhrim Guska's body spattered onto the ground, hacked in four. "Now!" Bulba shouted, and waved a scarf. Ostap understood his father's signal and, from where he lay in wait, lunged with his men toward the Polish cavalry. The Poles could not counter the powerful assault, and were pushed back toward the area in the field that Taras Bulba had fitted with broken spears and lances. Their horses staggered and fell, pitching their horsemen over their heads. The men of the Korsun Company, who were the last fighters to remain behind the carts, saw that the Poles had come within range, and began firing their muskets. The Poles collided with one another, their lines falling into complete disarray, and the Cossacks took heart once more. "Victory is ours!" Zaporozhian voices thundered. Bugles were sounded and flags raised. Maimed and mutilated Poles scurried over the field. "No, victory is not yet ours!" Taras Bulba shouted, looking toward the town's gates. And he was right.

The gates were flung open and a regiment of Hussars, the pride of the Polish cavalry, came galloping out. The horsemen were mounted on Asian Argamak steeds, and in front rode a knight more valiant and handsome than any of the others, his black curls flowing from beneath his burnished helmet. A precious scarf, embroidered by the loveliest of maidens, was tied to his arm. Taras saw with horror that it was Andri. Enveloped by the heat and dust of battle, thirsting to merit the gift tied to his arm, Andri came galloping like a young wolfhound, the handsomest, fastest, and youngest of the pack: a seasoned huntsman gives him a scent and the wolfhound goes tearing off, his paws a flat line in the air, his whole body leaning to the side, whipping up the snow, and in the heat of his sprint he outruns the hare tenfold. Taras reined in his horse and watched Andri cut his way through the Cossack lines, hacking at the men, his sword slashing left and right, sending the Cossacks running. "You are butchering your own people?"

Taras yelled, unable to restrain himself. "These are your own people, you devil's spawn!" But Andri could no longer tell what men were in front of him, whether they were his people or not. He could see nothing but locks of hair, long, beautiful locks, and a swan-white breast and a snow-white neck, and beautiful shoulders, all made for rapturous kisses.

"Men! Quick! Draw him over to the forest!" Taras shouted, and thirty of the swiftest Cossack riders set out to draw Andri to the forest. They pulled their tall lambskin hats tightly over their heads and galloped off on their steeds, cutting into the Hussars' riding path. The Cossacks attacked the first rows and sent them reeling, separating them from the rear, and giving more than one Hussar something to remember them by. Golokopitenko whipped Andri across the back with the flat of his sword, and then he and his men immediately galloped off at full Cossack speed. Andri flared up. The young blood surged in his veins. He dug his spurs into his horse's flanks and flew after the Cossacks, not looking back, not seeing that only twenty or so of his men had managed to follow him. The Cossacks raced on in full gallop and turned toward the forest, Andri close on their heels. He had almost caught up with Golokopitenko, when a strong hand suddenly grabbed his reins. Andri swerved around. Taras stood before him. A shudder ran through Andri's body, and his face turned ashen. Imagine a schoolboy elbowing a friend by mistake, and the friend viciously slapping him across the face: the outraged schoolboy flames up in anger and hurls himself at his startled friend, ready to tear him to pieces, when he suddenly bumps into the schoolmaster entering the class. In an instant his anger calms and his crazed rage subsides. Just like the schoolboy's rage, Andri's also disappeared in an instant, as if it had never existed. All he saw before him was the horrifying sight of his father.

"So, what are we going to do now?" Taras asked, looking him straight in the eye.

Andri did not know what to say, and sat on his horse with his eyes pinned to the ground.

"You did well by those Poles, didn't you?"

Andri remained silent.

"You betrayed us? Betrayed the faith? Betrayed your people? Get off your horse!"

Andri dismounted, obedient as a child, and stood before Taras more dead than alive.

"Don't move! I begot you and I shall kill you!" Taras said, and stepping back a pace, grabbed hold of the musket he was carrying slung across his shoulder.

Andri stood white as a shroud. His lips moved silently, as if uttering a name. But it was not the name of his native land, nor the name of his mother or his brother—it was the name of the beautiful Polish girl. Taras fired.

Like a sheaf of wheat cut by a scythe, like a calf feeling the fatal blade pierce its heart, Andri lowered his head and fell onto the grass without uttering a single word.

The father stared long at the lifeless body of the son he had murdered. Even in death he was beautiful: his manly face, recently filled with the strength and charm irresistible to women, was still filled with rare beauty. His black brows, like the somber velvet of grief, set off his pallid features.

"He would have made an excellent Cossack!" Taras said. "Tall, black-browed, with the face of a nobleman, and a powerful arm in battle! But he was lost to the Cossacks, lost in disgrace, like a vile dog!"

"Father! What have you done? Was it you who killed him?" Ostap shouted as he rode up.

Taras nodded.

Filled with pity, Ostap stared into his dead brother's eyes. "We must give him an honorable burial, Father, so that his body is not defiled by the enemy and the vultures will not tear him to shreds."

"Let the Poles bury him," Taras said. "There'll be plenty of mourners and wailers!"

Taras Bulba weighed whether he should throw Andri to the wolves, or whether he should honor his knightly prowess, which a valiant man esteems in another whether friend or foe. As he stood there, Golokopitenko came galloping toward him.

"A disaster, Ataman! The Poles have gained strength, new reinforcements have arrived!"

Golokopitenko had barely spoken when Vovtuzenko came galloping up.

"A disaster, Ataman! Even more enemy forces are gathering!"

Vovtuzenko had barely spoken when Pisarenko came running on foot, without his horse.

"Where have you been, Ataman? The Cossacks are looking for you! Captain Nevilichky has been killed, Zadorozhny has been killed, Cherevichenko has been killed! We are still holding out, but the men don't want to die without seeing you first. They want you to look into their eyes in their hour of death!"

"Onto your horse, Ostap!" Taras shouted, and rode off so that the Cossacks could see their Ataman in their final hour. But before Taras and Ostap could ride back out onto the field, the enemy forces had surrounded the forest, and horsemen with sabers and spears flashed between the trees. "Ostap! Ostap! Don't give yourself up!" Taras shouted, drawing his saber and wielding it at the men who were attacking him from all sides. Six Poles hurled themselves onto Ostap—to their great misfortune, as it turned out. One man's head flew off his shoulders, another man was felled as he tried to get away, and a third man's rib cage was pierced by Ostap's lance. A fourth man was more valiant, managing to dodge a fiery bullet, but the bullet plunged into his horse and the crazed animal toppled over and crushed him. "Good boy!" Taras shouted to Ostap, continuing to fight off the men who were attacking him. "Keep fighting, and I'll be right there!" Taras hacked and slashed, and many enemy heads rolled. He kept looking over to Ostap, who was being attacked by eight or nine more Poles. "Ostap! Ostap! Don't give yourself up!" But Ostap was already being overpowered. The Poles flung a noose around his neck, tied him with a rope, and dragged him away. "Ostap! Ostap!" Taras shouted, slashing at the men who were blocking his path. "Ostap! Ostap!" Suddenly Taras felt as if he had been hit by a heavy stone, and heads, spears, smoke, sparks of fire, twigs, and leaves flashed and reeled before his eyes as he tumbled to the ground like a felled oak. A thickening fog enveloped him.

10

"What a long time I have slept!" Taras muttered, waking as if from a drunken stupor. He stared at the unfamiliar objects around him. A terrible weakness weighed down his limbs. The walls and corners of the unknown room seemed to sway. He noticed his friend Tovkach sitting in front of him, apparently listening to every breath he took. "You fell asleep, and you might well have slept forever!" Tovkach was thinking. He did not say anything, but raised his finger sternly, motioning Taras to keep quiet.

"Where am I?" Taras asked him, straining his mind to remember what had happened.

"Quiet!" Tovkach shouted sharply. "Why do you want to know that? Can't you see you're covered in cuts and slashes? For two weeks I've been riding with you night and day, and you've been burning with fever, babbling nonsense! This is the first time you've slept peacefully. So just be quiet, that'll be far better!"

But Taras continued struggling to gather his thoughts and to remember what had happened. "Those damn Poles surrounded me and caught me! I couldn't have cut my way out!"

"Quiet, I said!" Tovkach shouted, angry as a nursemaid driven to despair by a child that will not sit still. "Why do you want to know how you got out of the fray? Isn't it good enough that you did? Some of us saw to it that the Poles didn't get you, and that's that! We have quite a few more nights of heavy riding in front of us! You are wrong if you think that the Poles see you as just another Cossack, they've put two thousand gold ducats on your head!"

"What about Ostap?" Taras shouted suddenly, trying to rise, remembering how he had seen Ostap captured and bound. Ostap had to be in the hands of the Poles.

Deep sorrow enveloped the old man. He tore off the bandages covering his wounds and flung them across the room. He wanted to say something, but began babbling nonsense again. Fever and delirium took over, and crazed, incoherent words flowed from him.

All the while, his faithful comrade stood in front of him, cursing in a stream of harsh reproaches. Finally he took Taras by the hands and feet, swaddled him like a baby, and bandaged him up again. He wrapped him in an ox hide, which he tied up with bast, fastening him onto the saddle with ropes, and they set off once more in a fast gallop. "Dead or alive, I'm going to get you back to the Sech! I won't let those damn Poles shame your Cossack pedigree, and tear your body to pieces and throw it in the river! And if an eagle is to rip out your eyes, then let it be an eagle of our steppes and not a damn Polish eagle, one that nests in Polish lands. Dead or alive, I am taking you back to the Ukraine!"

Those were the words of Taras's faithful comrade. He galloped night and day, Taras bound unconscious to his saddle, until they were back in the Zaporozhian Sech. There he set about curing Taras with herbs and compresses. Tovkach found a Jewess skilled in mixing potions, and for a whole month she plied Taras with medicines until he finally began to recover. Whether it was the potions that brought him back or his steely strength, a month and a half later he was on his legs again. His wounds healed, and only the saber scars bore witness to how severely he had been wounded. But he had become sullen and morose. Three deep furrows had dug their way into his forehead. Everything was new at the Sech. All his old comrades were dead. Not a single man was left who had fought for the true cause, for the faith, and for the brotherhood. The men who had set out with the former Ataman to hunt down the Tatars had also perished. They had all laid down their lives. Some had met valiant deaths in battle, others had died of hunger and thirst on the salt steppes of the Crimea, and others had perished in captivity, unable to bear the shame. The former Ataman had also died. All of Taras Bulba's old comrades were dead. Grass now grew over the brotherhood's seething strength. It was as if there had been a feast, a great, wild feast, and now all the cups and plates were lying in pieces, not a drop of wine was left, the servants and guests had stolen the precious chalices and goblets, and the host stood ruefully in the great hall wringing his hands, and cursing the day he had summoned all to carouse.

The Cossacks tried in vain to lift Taras's spirits. In vain did the gray-bearded bandura players walk in twos and threes singing the glory of his campaigns. He looked at everything with grim sullenness, an inextinguishable sorrow on his face. Hanging his head, he kept muttering, "My son! My Ostap!"

The Zaporozhians gathered for a sea campaign, and two hundred dugout skiffs were lowered into the Dnieper. Asia Minor saw the shorn and forelocked Cossacks ravage her flowering shores with sword and fire, and saw the turbans of its Mohammedan people floating in the shallows and strewn like myriad blossoms over its blood-drenched fields. It saw many tar-stained Cossack trousers, and muscular arms wielding black whips. The Zaporozhians devoured and trampled their way through the vineyards. They filled the mosques with piles of dung. They cut precious Persian shawls into foot wrappings and belts for their bespattered tunics. For a long time to come discarded Cossack pipes lay everwhere. The Zaporozhians set off to sail back home, but were pursued by a Turkish ten-gunner that fired salvos from all its cannons, dispersing their fragile skiffs like a flock of birds. A third of the skiffs were sunk, but the rest managed to regroup and make their way back to the mouth of the Dnieper with nineteen kegs filled with gold ducats. But all this no longer interested Taras. He rode out onto the steppes as if to hunt, but fired no shots. He sat despondently on the seashore, his gun next to him. He sat there for hours with his head hanging, muttering again and again, "My Ostap!" The Black Sea spread sparkling before him. A seagull cried in distant reeds. His white mustache gleamed silver, and tears fell one after the other.

Taras could bear it no longer. "Come what may, I must find out! Is he alive? Is he in his grave? Or wasn't he even buried? I must find out!"

A week later he rode into the town of Uman, armed with a lance and a saber, carrying a full supply of gunpowder, bullets, and horse harnesses, and with a water flask and a field kettle of kasha tied to his saddle. He rode up to a grimy little hovel with tiny soot-covered windows. The chimney was stopped up with rags, and the roof, leaking and full of holes, was covered with sparrows. A pile of litter lay in front of the door. The head of a Jewess in a cap with faded pearls poked out of a window.

"Is your husband at home?" Bulba asked, dismounting and tying his horse to an iron hook next to the door.

"Yes, he is," the Jewess said, and came hurrying out with a bucket of wheat for the horse and a mug of beer for Taras.

"Where is he?"

"He is in the front room, praying," the Jewess answered, bowing and wishing Taras good health as he raised the mug to his lips.

"I want you to stay here to feed and water my horse, while I go to talk to your husband in private. We have business to discuss."

The Jew Taras had come to see was none other than Yankel. He had already managed to set himself up in Uman as a leaseholder and tavern keeper, and had gradually managed to get all the surrounding Polish landowners and noblemen under his thumb, sucking them dry of all their money and firmly establishing his Jewish presence throughout the region. Every house within three miles was derelict, destitute, sold for drink. Poverty and rags were everywhere. The whole region was devastated as if ravaged by fire or plague, and were Yankel to live there another ten years the whole province would doubtless have been laid waste. Taras went into the front room. Yankel was praying, covered in a somewhat soiled prayer shawl. He turned to spit one last time, as is the custom in his faith, when he saw Bulba out of the corner of his eye. The first thing that flashed through the Jew's mind were the two thousand gold ducats on Bulba's head, but he felt shame at his greed and struggled to stifle his eternal craving for gold, which like a serpent encircles the soul of every Jew.

"I saved your life!" Taras said to Yankel, who had begun bowing before him, carefully locking the door so they would not be overheard. "Had it not been for me, the Zaporozhians would have torn you to pieces like a dog. Now it is your turn to do me a favor!"

The Jew's face puckered up. "What favor? Well, if there's a favor a man can do, why shouldn't he do it?"

"Enough talk. Take me to Warsaw."

"To Warsaw? What do you mean, take you to Warsaw?" Yankel asked, raising his shoulders and eyebrows in astonishment.

"Enough talk. Just take me to Warsaw. I want to see him one more time, to say at least one last word to him."

"Say one last word to whom?"

"To him, to Ostap, my son!"

"But doesn't Your Excellency know that—"

"I know, I know everything: there's two thousand gold ducats on my head! As if those fools know what my head is worth! I'll give you five thousand. Here's two thousand now!" Bulba poured two thousand ducats out of his leather bag. "You'll get the rest when we come back."

The Jew grabbed a rag and quickly covered the ducats with it. "Oy, what magnificent money! Oy, what good money!" he crooned, twirling a ducat between his fingers and biting it to see if it was real. "I am sure that the man from whom Your Excellency took these marvelous ducats could not have survived their loss by more than an hour—that very same hour he must have gone down to the river and drowned himself for such marvelous ducats!"

"I wouldn't have asked you—I'm sure I could have made my way to Warsaw myself. But it wouldn't surprise me if those cursed Poles somehow recognized me, as I'm not good at tricks and ruses. But you Jews are made for that sort of thing! You could hoodwink the devil himself! You know all the tricks, and this is why I came to you. Even if I made my way to Warsaw on my own, I'm sure I couldn't manage things once I was there. So get the cart ready and take me there!"

"And Your Excellency thinks that I can simply harness my mare and shout, 'Off we go now, Sivka!' You think I can take you there just like that without even hiding you?"

"Well then, hide me! Hide me anywhere you want! How about in an empty barrel?"

"Oy vey! You think I can hide you in an empty barrel? Don't you know that the first thing people think when they see a barrel is that it's filled with vodka?"

"So what if they think it's filled with vodka?"

"So what if they think it's filled with vodka?" the Jew gasped, clasping his sidelocks and throwing both hands in the air.

"Well?"

"Don't you know that God put vodka on this earth for everyone to taste? The whole place is teeming with greedy hogs and lushes. A Pole wouldn't think twice about running five versts after a cart to bore a little hole into a barrel, and when he sees that nothing comes trickling out he'll say, 'Hey, that Jew can't just be driving an empty barrel around for nothing! Something fishy must be going on! Catch the Jew! Tie up the Jew! Take away all the Jew's money! Throw the Jew in jail!' And all this because everything bad is always rained down on a Jew's head, because everyone takes a Jew for a dog! Because everyone thinks a Jew is not a human being!"

"So why not hide me in a cartload of fish?"

"I cannot do that! Everywhere in Poland people are starving like dogs—they'll steal the fish and there you'll be, lying in the cart for everyone to see!"

"Then get me there on the devil's back, damn it, but just get me there!"

"Maybe we can do something," the Jew suddenly said, rolling up his sleeves and walking up to Taras with his arms spread wide. "This is what we'll do. The Poles are building fortresses and palaces all over the place. French engineers have been coming in from the German duchies, and so bricks and stones are being carted over all the roads. What we can do is have you lie down in the cart and stack a pile of bricks over you. You look strong enough, so you won't mind if it is a little heavy. And I'll cut a hole in the bottom of the cart so I can feed you."

"Do whatever you want, just get me there!"

An hour later, two mares pulled a cart loaded with bricks out of Uman. Lanky Yankel was sitting on one of the mares, his long curly sidelocks hanging from under his yarmulke and swaying as he sat bobbing on the saddle, long and thin as a verst marker by the roadside.

11

Along the borders in those days there were no customs officials or guards, the terror and bane of every enterprising man, and anyone could bring across anything they wanted. If someone should undertake a search or inspection, it was more for personal pleasure, particularly if a cart was carrying tempting items and the man's fist had the necessary weight and punch. The bricks, however, found no admirers, and so went without hindrance through the town's main gates. Locked in his tight cage, Bulba could see nothing; he only heard the din and the yells of the carters in the streets. Yankel, bobbing up and down on his small, muddy horse, made a few detours through the streets of the town, and then pulled into a dark, narrow back alley, called Dirt Street or Jew Street, because Jews from all over Warsaw lived there. The alley looked like a backyard that had been turned inside out. It was as if the sun never shone there. The grimy wooden houses and the masses of clothes poles sticking out their windows made the alley even darker. Here and there the red shimmer of brick glimmered through, but most of the walls were completely covered in grime.

Rarely, a plastered stretch of wall high up, seized by the sun, glared with blinding whiteness. Everything lay in a jumble: pipes, rags, rotting peels, broken tubs. All the waste and refuse was thrown into the street, assailing the senses of the passersby. A man on horseback could practically touch the clothes poles stretching across the alley from one house to another, on which hung Jewish stockings, short pantaloons, and smoked geese. Sometimes the pretty face of a Jewess, decorated with faded beads, peered out a tiny, decrepit window. A swarm of mud-smeared, tattered urchins with curly hair was yelling and wallowing about in the dirt. A red-haired Jew, his face packed with freckles like a sparrow's egg, was looking out a window and began talking to Yankel in their gibberish, and Yankel drove the cart into one of the courtyards. Another passing Jew joined their conversation, and when Bulba pulled himself out from under the heap of bricks he saw three Jews immersed in a heated debate.

Yankel turned to Bulba and told him that everything would be taken care of. Ostap was in the town jail, and though it would be hard to convince the guards, Yankel hoped that he would be able to arrange a meeting.

Bulba went into the house with the three Jews, who again began talking in their incomprehensible language. Taras stared at them. He was gripped by strong emotion. His rough, callous face was touched with the flame of hope—the kind of hope that sometimes grips a man in the depths of despair. His old heart began beating with the vigor of youth. "There's nothing on earth you Jews cannot do!" he gasped ecstatically. "If there's something lying on the bottom of the sea, you will find a way to bring it up. As the proverb says: When a Jew has the will to rob, he will rob himself if he has to! Free my son Ostap! Give him a chance to escape from the devil's hands! I have promised Yankel twelve thousand ducats—I will double that! Everything I have, from the most precious chalices to the treasure I have buried, everything, my house, the clothes off my back, I will sell everything, and sign a contract that I will give you half of all the spoils of war I will henceforth lay my hands on!"

"Oh, we cannot do that, Your Excellency, we cannot," Yankel said with a sigh.

"No, we cannot!" the second Jew agreed.

The three Jews eyed one another.

"Well, we *could* try, couldn't we?" the third Jew said, looking at the other two with frightened eyes. "With God's help, you never know!"

The three Jews began speaking in German. Bulba strained his ears, but could only catch the word "Mordechai," which the men often repeated.

"Listen, Your Excellency!" Yankel said. "We have to seek advice from a man the likes of whom the world has never seen. Oy, is he a wise man, wise as Solomon, and if he cannot do a thing, then nobody can do it. Stay here and wait for us. Here is the key, and don't let anyone in!"

The three Jews left. Taras locked the door and looked out the window into the dirty alley. The Jews stopped in the middle of the alley and began talking excitedly. They were joined by a fourth man, and then a fifth. Taras again heard "Mordechai, Mordechai." The Jews kept looking toward one end of the street, where finally a foot in a Jewish slipper and the folds of a short caftan came poking out of a ramshackle little house. "Ah, Mordechai, Mordechai!" the Jews shouted. A gaunt Jew, somewhat shorter than Yankel but a good deal more wrinkled, and with an astonishingly large upper lip, came toward the impatient crowd, and all the Jews, interrupting one another, hurried to tell him everything. Mordechai kept looking over to the small window, and Taras guessed that they were talking about him. Mordechai waved his hands, listened, interrupted the others, often spat to the side, lifting the folds of his caftan and revealing his filthy pants as he rummaged about in his pockets, pulling out all kinds of trinkets. Finally the crowd was shouting so loud that the Jew standing watch had to motion them to keep quiet. Taras began to worry for his safety, but then remembered that Jews always discussed matters in the street, and that the devil himself could not understand their language.

A few minutes later the Jews came crowding into the room. Mordechai walked up to Taras, patted him on the shoulder, and said, "When man and God want to do something, then it will be done!"

Taras looked at this Solomon, the likes of whom the world had never seen, and a glimmer of hope sparked within him. Mordechai's appearance did somehow inspire confidence. It was clear that his upper lip was nothing more than an intimidating decoy, and that its thickness had been increased by beatings. This Solomon's beard consisted of only fifteen hairs, on the left side. On his face were so many signs of the beatings he had received for his audacity that he had doubtless lost count of them, and thought of the scars as birthmarks.

Mordechai left the room with his friends, who were brimming over with wonder at his wisdom. Bulba stayed back alone. He was in a strange state of mind. He was worried for the first time in his life. His soul was in feverish turmoil. He was no longer the unbending, unshakable man, powerful as an oak tree. He had become fainthearted. Weak. He trembled at every sound, at every Jewish silhouette that appeared at the end of the street. He spent the whole day in this state. He didn't eat, didn't drink, and kept his eyes pinned on the little window that looked out onto the alley.

Finally, late in the evening, Mordechai and Yankel returned. Taras's heart stopped. "Well? Any luck?" he asked with the impatience of a wild steed. But before the Jews could catch their breath, Taras saw that the two men had been badly roughed up, and that Mordechai was now missing the last few wisps of hair that had hung in an oily tangle from under his yarmulke. Mordechai started talking so incoherently that Taras could not understand a word.

"Oh, Your Excellency!" Yankel gasped, holding his hand over his battered mouth as if he had caught a cold. "It is completely impossible! By God, it is impossible! Those Poles are so evil that they deserve that their heads be spat upon. Mordechai will tell you the same thing. Mordechai did what no man in the world has managed to do, but God did not want this to be. They are holding three thousand Cossacks there, and tomorrow they will all be put to death!"

Taras looked the Jews in the eyes, but no longer with impatience or anger.

"And if Your Excellency wants to see him, then tomorrow he has to go early, before the sun has even risen. The watchmen have agreed, and one of the foremen has promised to let us in. But may they find no happiness on this earth! Oy, vey iz mir! What a greedy race these Poles are! You'd never find a Jew like that! I had to pay fifty ducats, and the foreman—"

"Good! Take me to him!" Taras said decisively, resolve pouring back into his soul.

He agreed with Yankel's suggestion that he dress up as a foreign count, a visitor from a German principality, and Yankel, with his customary foresight, had already arranged for the clothes. Night had fallen. The master of the house, the freckled, red-haired Jew, pulled out a tattered mattress with a bast covering and laid it out on a bench for Bulba. Yankel lay down on the floor on a similar mattress. The red-haired Jew drank a small mug of some sort of brew, took off his caftan—in his stockings and slippers looking somewhat like a chicken—and climbed with his Jewess into what looked like a cupboard. Two children lay on the floor next to the cupboard like little house dogs. But Taras did not sleep. He sat motionless by the table, his fingers drumming lightly. His pipe was in his mouth and he blew out smoke, which made the Jew sneeze in his sleep and dig his nose deeper into the covers. Before the pale harbingers of dawn even touched the sky, Taras nudged Yankel with his foot.

"Get up, Jew, and give me those count's clothes!"

He was dressed in a minute. He darkened his mustache and brows, and put on a small black hat. His oldest Cossack comrades would not have recognized him. He did not look a day over thirty-five. A healthy flush played on his cheeks, and even the scars on his face added to his majestic air. The clothes with their gold trimmings suited him well.

The streets were still asleep. In the town not a single merchant had yet appeared carrying a box or pushing a cart. Bulba and Yankel came to a huge building that looked like a crouching heron. It was low, wide, and sooty, and from one of its sides a long thin gabled tower rose like the neck of a swan. This building fulfilled a number of functions, housing the barracks, the prison, and even the criminal court. Taras and Yankel entered the gates and found themselves in the middle of a wide hall, actually a covered courtyard, in which almost a thousand Polish soldiers were sleeping side by side. There was a low door at the far end, in front of which watchmen sat playing a game in which one of them was trying to hit the palm of the other with two fingers. They paid no attention to the new arrivals, and only looked up when Yankel said, "We have come, gentlemen! It's us!"

"You can go inside," one of the guards said, opening the door with one hand, holding out the other for his friend to hit.

Taras and Yankel entered a narrow dark corridor, which led them to another hall much like the first, with small windows high up.

"Who goes there?" some voices called, and Taras saw a large number of royal guardsmen in full armor. "Our orders are to let nobody through!"

"It's us!" Yankel shouted. "It's us, illustrious gentlemen!"

The guardsmen would not listen, but fortunately a corpulent man happened to walk in who seemed to be their chief, for he cursed louder and more roughly than any of the others.

"It's us, you know us already, and His Excellency the count will express his gratitude to you with great generosity!"

"Let them pass, you pack of devils! But let no one else through! And I don't want to see nobody take his saber off so he can curl up on the floor like some flea-bitten dog, or else . . ." Taras and Yankel did not hear the end of the grandiloquent order.

"It's us!"—"It's me!"—"We're friends!" Yankel kept repeating to all and sundry.

"Can we go in now?" he asked one of the watchmen, when they came to the end of the corridor.

"Yes, you can. Only . . . I don't know if they'll let you into the actual prison. Jan isn't there anymore, another man's taken over," the watchman said.

"Oy, oy!" Yankel gasped. "What a terrible blow!"

"Take me in anyway!" Taras said gruffly.

Yankel obeyed.

In front of the door to the cellar stood a royal guardsman with a three-tiered mustache. The upper tier pointed backward, the middle tier straight ahead, and the lower tier pointed down, which gave him a remarkably catlike air. Yankel sidled over to him, bowing and scraping. "Your Excellency! Most illustrious gentleman!"

"Is it me you are talking to, Jew?"

"Oh yes, most illustrious gentleman!"

"Hmm . . . Well, I'm just a simple guardsman!" the man with the three-tiered mustache said, a twinkle of pleasure in his eye.

"A guardsman? And I thought you were the governor himself, ai, ai, ai!" Yankel crooned, wagging his head and throwing his hands up in disbelief. "But you look so stately! I would have sworn that you were at least a colonel, at least! Were one to put you on a horse fast as lightning you would cut a fine figure reviewing your regiments!"

The guardsman smoothed the lower tier of his mustache, his eyes now sparkling with delight.

"What fine military figures all you Poles are!" the Jew continued. "Oy, vey iz mir, what fine military figures! All those trimmings and emblems, they shine like the sun! And when the girls see military men like you, oy, oy!"

The Jew again wagged his head.

The guardsman twirled the upper tier of his mustache, and a sound not unlike that of a horse neighing came bursting from between his teeth.

"May I ask the illustrious gentleman for a favor?" Yankel asked. "His Excellency the Prince here is visiting from a foreign country and would like to take a look at some Cossacks, because in all his life he has never set eyes on one!"

In those days it was quite common for foreign barons and counts to visit Poland, drawn by the thrill of seeing a half-Asiatic corner of Europe. In their view, Muscovy and the Ukraine were completely Asiatic. Therefore the guardsman, with a deep bow, felt it appropriate to add a few words of his own. "It is beyond me, Your Illustrious Excellency, why you would be interested in taking a look at Cossacks. Cossacks are dogs, not men! And as for their faith, it is scorned by all the world!"

"You are lying, you devil's spawn!" Bulba exploded. "It is you who are a dog! How can you say that our faith is scorned when it is your own heretical faith that is despised by all!"

"Aha!" the guardsman shouted. "Now I see what you are, my friend! You are one and the same with those dogs I'm guarding in there! Halt! I'm calling in my men!"

Taras immediately realized what his outburst had led to, but his stubbornness and fury kept him from finding a way of setting things right. Fortunately, Yankel managed to jump in.

"Most illustrious gentleman! How would it be possible for His Excellency the Count to be a Cossack? If he were a Cossack, how would he have gotten hold of such garments and such a princely air?"

"Don't try to hoodwink me!" the guardsman barked, and opened his mouth wide to call the other guards.

"No, no, Your Majestic Excellency!" Yankel squealed. "We shall reward you with money like you have never seen before! We shall give you two gold ducats!"

"Two ducats! What are two lousy ducats to me? I give my barber two ducats to shave a single cheek! Give me a hundred ducats, Jew!" The guardsman twirled the upper tier of his mustache. "If you don't give me a hundred ducats, I shall call the others right away!"

"Why so much?" the ashen Jew muttered sorrowfully, opening his leather pouch, overjoyed that there was not more than a hundred ducats inside, and that the guardsman was obviously unable to count above a hundred. But Yankel noted that the guardsman was counting the coins with an ominous air of regret that he had not asked for more.

"Quickly, Your Excellency, we had better leave! You can see what dreadful people these are!" he said.

"You damn devil!" Bulba shouted at the guardsman. "You've taken the money, and now you won't show us the prisoners? You've got to show them! You've taken the money, so you've no right to turn us down!"

"Get out of here! Get out of here, damn you, or else I'll call the others right away! Get out of here! Out!"

"Let us go, let us go! A plague upon him! May he see dreams that will make him spit!" poor Yankel shouted.

Bulba slowly turned around and walked off with lowered head, followed by the reproaches of Yankel, who was devoured by grief over the wasted ducats. "Why did you have to start quarreling with him? You should have let the dog curse all he wanted! That's the kind of people they are—all they do is curse! Oy vey iz mir! The luck God sends to some people on this earth! A hundred gold ducats just to chase us away! And what do we Jews get? Our sidelocks ripped out and our faces punched until people have to look away in disgust! Oh God! Oh merciful God!"

But this mishap had a far more profound effect on Bulba. An all-consuming flame burned in his eyes.

"Let's go!" he suddenly said, as if shaking himself out of a stupor. "Let's go to the main square. I want to watch them torture him."

"Oy, why go there? How can that help him?"

"We'll go!" Bulba said obstinately, and the Jew, sighing, trotted behind him like an anxious nursemaid.

The square on which the execution was to take place was not hard to find: the whole town was streaming there from all directions. In that grim bygone era an execution was considered one of the most engaging spectacles, not only for the masses but also for the aristocracy. Devout old women, matrons, and timid young girls refused to pass up the opportunity to satisfy their curiosity, though they would afterward dream all night of blood-drenched corpses and shout in their sleep as only drunken Hussars can. On the square, many were to call out in feverish hysteria, "Oh, how they torture them!" covering their eyes and turning away, and yet none were prepared to forgo the gruesome spectacle. Others stared with open mouths and craning necks, ready to clamber onto their neighbors' backs to get a better view. From the crowd of humdrum haggard faces a butcher stuck out his meaty jowls, watching the whole procedure with the eyes of a connoisseur, exchanging one-word comments with a swordsmith he called brother because the two got drunk in the same tavern. Some spectators were arguing hotly, others were even placing bets, but most were the sort of people who pick their noses as they stare absently at the world and everything in it. In the foreground, next to the mustachioed police guard, stood a young nobleman or would-be nobleman dressed in military garb, who was wearing every piece of finery he owned, so that all he had left behind in his rooms was a torn shirt and an old pair of shoes. Two gold chains, one above the other, hung around his neck, some sort of ducat dangling from one of them. He was with his sweetheart, Jozefka, and staring nervously in all directions, worried that someone might sully her silk dress. He was explaining everything to her in such detail that one would have been hard put to add anything more. "My darling Jozefka, all these people have come to watch the criminals being executed. The man standing over there, my sweet— the one who is holding the ax and the other instruments—is the executioner who will chop their heads off. When he puts the criminal on the wheel and starts torturing him the criminal is still alive, but when he chops his head off, my sweet„ then the criminal is dead. At first you will see the criminal writhing and shouting, but once his head has been chopped off he won't be able to shout, or eat, or drink. This, my sweet, is because he won't have a head anymore." And Jozefka listened with a mix of fear and excitement.

The roofs of the houses were brimming with people. Strange faces with mustaches and head coverings that resembled old women's nightcaps peered from dormer windows. The aristocracy sat on canopied balconies. A laughing young woman's pretty hand, sparkling like the purest sugar, rested on a railing. Grand and portly gentlemen looked on with an important air. A servant in rich livery with elegant folded-back sleeves was serving an array of delicacies and wines. Often one feisty dark-browed maiden snatched up a piece of pastry or fruit, which she flung into a crowd of hungry knights holding out their hats, and a tall gallant in a faded red tunic with threadbare gold trimmings craned his head above the rest and made good use of his long arms to catch the prize, press it to his heart and stuff it into his mouth. A falcon in a golden cage that hung beneath one of the balconies was also a spectator: inclining its beak to the side and raising one of its claws it carefully watched the spectacle. The crowd suddenly stirred, and voices rose from all sides, "The Cossacks! They are bringing the Cossacks!"

They were led onto the square, their heads bare and their forelocks and beards in tangles. They were not sullen, but had an air of quiet pride. Their garments of precious cloth were threadbare, and hung from them like tattered rags. They did not look at the crowd. Ostap was walking in front.

What did Taras feel when he saw his son Ostap? What was in his heart at that moment? He looked at him from the crowd, not missing a single movement. They approached the executioner's platform. Ostap stopped. It fell to him to be the first to drink from the bitter cup. He looked at his brothers, raised his hand, and loudly proclaimed, "God grant that all the profane heretics gathered here will not see a single true Christian Cossack succumb to torture and cry out in weakness!"

Ostap walked up to the scaffold.

"Good, my son, good!" Bulba said quietly, and lowered his gray head.

The executioner pulled off the rags Ostap was wearing. His hands and legs were tied to the torture rack and . . . But I shall not distress my readers with the image of the hellish, hair-raising torture prevalent in that grim era in which man, living a blood-drenched life of military campaigns, tempered his soul by stifling his humanity. A few free-thinking men had protested these terrible measures, but to no avail. The King and many of his knights, enlightened in mind and soul, had asserted that such cruel punishment could only incur the vengeance of the Cossack nation. But the power of the King and his wise advisers could not withstand the insolent will of the reigning feudal magnates, who with their recklessness, lack of foresight, selfishness, and foolish arrogance turned the Polish parliament into a mockery of government. Ostap bore the torment and agony heroically, not emitting a single cry, even when the bones of his arms and legs began to break with terrible loud cracks that echoed through the silent crowd to the far end of the square, young ladies averting their eyes in horror. His face remained impassive, and not a sound escaped his lips. Taras stood in the crowd with lowered head, raising his eyes from time to time and muttering proudly, "Good, my son, good!"

Yet when Ostap was submitted to the final fatal torture it seemed as if his resolve might falter. He looked at the crowd. God, nothing but unknown faces! If only someone close could stand by him as he faced death! He did not want the sobs and wailing of a weak mother, or the crazed howls of a bride tearing her hair and beating her breast. He wanted a strong man to stand by him, someone who could strengthen him with a sound word, comforting him as he breathed his last. Ostap's resolve abandoned him and he shouted, "Father, where are you? Can you hear me?"

"I can hear you!" Taras's voice echoed from the silent crowd, sending a shudder through the myriad men and women in the square.

The mounted guardsmen immediately began combing through the masses. Yankel's face was white as death. The horsemen made their way past him, and he turned around in terror to look at Taras, but Taras had disappeared without a trace.

12

And yet Taras was to reappear. A hundred and twenty thousand Cossack warriors marched across the Ukrainian border. This time the force was not made up just of some regiments, or a fraction of the Cossack army riding out for plunder or to hunt after the Tatars. The Cossack people had finally been tried beyond endurance, and the whole nation rose to seek vengeance for the denial of its rights, the disgracing of its customs, the affront to its holy rituals and faith, the desecration of its churches, the excesses of the Polish masters, the oppression, the enforced union with Poland, the shameful dominion of Jews on Christian soil—everything that for generations had fanned the grim hatred of the Cossacks. The young, spirited Hetman Ostranitsa led the massive Cossack forces. At his side rode Gunya, his veteran war-tried comrade and adviser. Eight colonels led a regiment of twelve thousand men each. Two major generals and the staff-bearer general rode behind the Hetman. A cornet carried the main banner. Many more flags and banners fluttered in the distance. Ordinary staff bearers were carrying the staffs of the captains of each company. There were many other regimental ranks—the ranks of the cart divisions, the regular ranks, the ranks of regimental scribes—and with them infantry and cavalry detachments. Among the Cossacks there were almost as many volunteers as enlisted men. They had come together from throughout the nation, from Chigirin, Pereyaslav, Baturin, Glukhov; from the lower and upper Dnieper regions and the river islands. Countless horses and an eternal procession of carts advanced over the fields. Among the eight regiments of twelve thousand men one was finer than all the rest: the regiment led by Taras Bulba. He had many advantages over the other colonels: his age, his experience in war, his flair for inspiring his men, but above all, his unmatched hatred for the enemy. Even the Cossacks were stunned by his ruthless brutality. His speeches in the war council called for destruction, nothing but destruction, and the only sentence he passed on enemy captives was the death by gallows or the stake.

There is no point in describing the many battles in which the Cossacks distinguished themselves, nor the progression of the campaign. All this can be read in the pages of the chronicles. It is common knowledge how a war for the faith is waged on Russian soil—no earthly power is stronger than the power of faith. It is insurmountable and ferocious, like a rock rising from the depths of a stormy ocean, fashioned from a single unshatterable mass of stone, towering into the skies, seen from vast distances and glaring at the waves that roll past. And woe unto the ship that is hurled onto this rock! Its rigging will be torn to shreds as the ship shatters and sinks with all hands, the battered wind resounding with the piteous cries of the drowning men.

The pages of the chronicles describe in detail how the Polish garrisons fled the liberated towns, how the unscrupulous Jewish leaseholders were hanged, how weak the puppet Hetman of the Polish crown, Nikolai Potocki, was against the unstoppable Cossack forces, notwithstanding his powerful army. Beaten and pursued, Potocki drove his men into a small river where most of them drowned, and he sought refuge in the town of Polonne, where the ruthless Cossack regiments besieged him. Driven to desperation, Potocki pledged a solemn oath that the Polish King and his parliament would meet all the Cossack demands, and that all the Cossacks' former sovereign rights would be restored. The Cossacks were not to be duped by empty promises, for they knew what a Polish oath was worth, but the Russian clergy in Polonne saved Potocki. Had they not come to his rescue, he would never again have paraded in splendor on his six-thousand-ducat Argamak steed, drawing the glances of the most fashionable ladies and the envy of the nobility, nor would he have caused excitement at the Polish parliament, throwing lavish feasts for the senators. The priests came out of the town in their radiant golden cassocks, carrying icons and crosses, the Archimandrite in front of the procession bearing a cross and the holy shepherd's miter. The Cossacks removed their hats and bowed their heads. They would not have shown such respect to anyone lower than the King, but they showed full reverence before the True Church and its priesthood. The Cossack Hetman Ostranitsa and his colonels agreed to release Potocki after they took from him the solemn oath to leave the churches of the True Faith unharmed, to forget the old enmity, and never again to march against the Cossack army. There was only one colonel who did not agree to such a peace—Taras Bulba. He tore a lock of hair from his head and shouted, "Hetman and Brother Colonels! Turn your backs on this fainthearted, womanish deal! Do not trust the cursed Poles, the dogs will deceive us!"

When the regimental scribe announced the conditions and the Hetman officially seconded them, Taras Bulba unsheathed the clean Damascus steel of his precious Turkish sword, broke it in two like a reed, and flung the pieces far in opposite directions. "Farewell! Just as the two ends of that blade will never again be joined into one, we too, comrades, will never see each other again in this world! Remember my parting words!" Here his voice rose, grew, and took on unprecedented power; all the men were deeply struck by his prophetic words. "You will remember me at your hour of death! You think that you have just bought yourself a little peace and tranquillity! You think that you will be the masters now! But you will not be the masters! The Poles will peel the skin off your head, Hetman Ostranitsa, and fill it with buckwheat, and it will be paraded for a long time to come at markets and fairs! And you, comrades, will not keep your heads on your shoulders either! You will die immured in the stone walls of cold cellars, if they don't stick you in large cauldrons and boil you alive!" And turning to his regiment he shouted, "Men! Who among you wants to die a valiant death, and not a death huddled by the stove like an old woman, or dead drunk in a tavern yard like carrion! An honorable Cossack death, all in the same bed, like brides and bridegrooms, in the great bed of the battlefield! Or do you want to go back home and turn into nonbelievers, and bow and scrape before the Polish priests?"

"We will march with you, Colonel!" all the men in his regiment shouted, and many men from other regiments pledged their allegiance, too.

"If you will march with me, then let us march!" Taras shouted. He pulled his hat tightly over his head, glared grimly at the men who stayed behind, righted himself in his saddle, and called out: "Let no one dare insult us as we ride away! Men! We are going to pay those Catholics a visit!"

He rode off, and a procession of a hundred carts rolled after him, followed by many Cossack horsemen and foot soldiers. Bulba turned and stared grimly at the Cossacks who were staying behind, and anger raged in his eyes. No one dared make a move to stop Taras and his men, and for a long time Taras glared back in threateningly.

The Hetman and his colonels looked on, deeply troubled. They stood silent and lost in thought, as if weighed down by a heavy presentiment. And Taras's prophesies had not missed their mark. Everything he foretold came to pass. The Poles were soon to break their word, and they launched an attack on the Cossacks at Kanev, and the Hetman's head was stuck on a pole, as were those of many of the town's foremost dignitaries.

And what happened to Taras? Taras tore through Poland with his regiment, burning down eighteen towns, and close to forty Catholic churches, and pushing forward as far as Krakow. He slaughtered many Polish noblemen and plundered the most magnificent and wealthy castles, smashing barrels and spilling rare wines and meads that had been jealously guarded in noblemen's cellars. The Cossacks tore and burned precious cloths and garments, and smashed the delicate plate-ware they found in cupboards. "Spare nothing!" Taras told his men again and again. The Cossacks did not even spare the dark-browed Polish beauties, white-breasted virgins with radiant countenances, who found no refuge, not even in churches as they clung to altars. Taras ordered them to be burnt along with the altars. Many arms, white as snow, reached out to the sky from the flames, with cries piteous enough to move the cold earth and make the grasses of the steppes bend low in sorrow at their terrible fate. But the cruel Cossacks were not moved. In the street they speared infants with their lances and hurled them to their mothers in the flames. "You cursed Poles! This is a memorial service for Ostap!" was all Taras said. And he held such memorial services for Ostap in every town and village he came upon, until the Polish parliament realized that Bulba's attacks were not just Cossack raids, and Potocki was sent out in person with five regiments to capture him.

For six days the Cossacks fled Potocki's pursuit by galloping down distant country roads. The horses saved the Cossacks, though they could hardly bear the unremitting gallop. This time Potocki proved worthy of his task. He pursued the Cossacks relentlessly and caught up with them on the riverbanks of the Dniester, where Bulba had occupied a crumbling, abandoned fortress in order to rest his troops.

The fortress loomed over the river with its breached rampart and crumbling walls. The cliff on which it stood was heaped with broken bricks and shattered stone slabs ready to come tumbling down at any moment. It was here that Potocki, the puppet Hetman of the Polish crown, cornered Taras Bulba, blocking the two sides of the fortress that opened out to the fields. For four days the Cossacks fought off the Poles, hurling down bricks and stones. But their supplies and strength began to wane, and Taras decided to fight his way through Potocki's lines. And the Cossacks had almost fought their way through, and perhaps their swift horses would once again have served them faithfully, but Taras stopped in mid-gallop and shouted, "Halt! I dropped my tobacco pipe! I am leaving nothing for the Poles, not even my pipe!" And the old Ataman stooped down to the grass to look for his pipe, his true companion on land and water, on the battlefield and in his home. At that moment a band of Poles descended upon him and grabbed him by his mighty shoulders. He writhed and struggled with all his might, but the Poles did not topple from their horses as they had always done in the past. "Old age, cursed old age!" he gasped, and the hefty Cossack began to weep. But old age was not to blame. His strength was overpowered by a superior force: almost thirty Poles clung to his arms and legs.

"We have caught the blackguard!" they shouted. "Now we must settle on which of the highest honors we can accord the dog!"

They decided with Hetman Potocki's permission that Taras should be burnt in full view of his men. A bare tree stood nearby, its top shattered by lightning. They tied him to the trunk with chains, high up so he could be seen from afar. They hammered nails into his hands, and began building a fire at the foot of the tree. But Taras did not look down at the fire, nor did he give a second thought to the flames that were to burn him. He was looking in the direction where the Cossacks were battling the Poles: from where he was he could see all the positions clearly.

"Men! Quick! Head for the hill behind the woods!" he shouted. "They won't be able to get at you there!"

But the wind did not carry his words to the Cossacks.

"They will die for nothing, for nothing!" he cried in desperation, and looked down at the sparkling waters of the Dniester. Joy flamed up in his eyes. He saw four skiffs moored behind some bushes. He mustered his strength and called out with all his might, "Men! To the riverbank! Head down the hillside path to your left! There are skiffs on the bank! Take them and flee!"

This time the wind was blowing from the other side, and the Cossacks heard Taras's words. For shouting to his comrades he was given a blow on the head with a musket butt, sending everything swirling before his eyes.

The Cossacks rode at full gallop down the hillside path, with their pursuers close on their heels. They saw that the path wound down the slope with many bends. "Comrades! All or nothing!" they shouted, reining in their horses for an instant at the edge of the cliff. Then they raised their whips and whistled, and their Tatar steeds bounded into the air, unfurled like snakes, flew over the precipice, and tumbled into the Dniester. Only two men did not reach the river. They toppled from the cliff onto the rocks, perishing with their horses before they could even emit a cry. The other Cossacks swam with their horses through the river and untied the skiffs. The Poles stopped by the edge of the cliff, amazed at the Cossacks' unprecedented feat, and wondered whether they should follow their example. A young colonel, a hot-blooded youth—the brother of the beautiful Polish girl who had beguiled poor Andri—did not ponder long, and with all his might he plunged with his horse after the Cossacks. He turned three times in the air and tumbled onto the rocks below, their sharp edges tearing him to pieces, his blood and brains spattering the bushes that grew along the jagged walls of the ravine.

When Taras regained consciousness after the blow he had received, he looked at the Dniester where the Cossacks were already rowing away in the skiffs. Bullets rained down on them from above, but did not reach them. The old Ataman's eyes sparkled with joy.

"Farewell, comrades!" he shouted to them. "Remember me, and come back next spring to feast and carouse! So you thought you'd caught us, you damn Poles? Do you think there is a single thing in this world that will frighten a Cossack? Just wait, the time will come when you will understand the meaning of the Russian Orthodox faith! Word has already spread through every nation: A Russian Czar will spring forth from the Russian earth, and there will be no power in this world that shall not yield to him!"

The fire began to rise, and snatched at his feet as the flames spread up the tree. But is there fire, torture, or force powerful enough in all the world to subjugate the Russian spirit?

Wide is the River Dniester, and many are its bays, thick beds of reed, sandbanks, and depths. The river's mirror sparkles, filled with the ringing call of swans, and a proud golden-eye soars above, and the reeds and riverbanks are filled with sandpipers and red-beaked snipes. The Cossacks rowed swiftly over the waters in the narrow two-ruddered skiffs, dipping the oars in smooth rhythm, carefully skirting the sandbanks from which frightened birds fluttered, and they remembered their Ataman.

ABOUT THE TRANSLATOR

PETER CONSTANTINE was awarded the 1998 PEN Translation Award for his translation of *Six Early Stories* by Thomas Mann and the 1999 National Translation Award for his translation of *The Undiscovered Chekhov: Forty-three New Stories*, and has been widely acclaimed for his recent translation of the complete works of Isaac Babel. He lives in New York City.

THE MODERN LIBRARY EDITORIAL BOARD

A NOTE ON THE TYPE

The principal text of this Modern Library edition
was set in a digitized version of Janson, a typeface that
dates from about 1690 and was cut by Nicholas Kis,
a Hungarian working in Amsterdam. The original matrices have
survived and are held by the Stempel foundry in Germany.
Hermann Zapf redesigned some of the weights and sizes for
Stempel, basing his revisions on the original design.